# *Dark Pr*

## *Unmasking Pr* ...

# **Book 5**

# **By**

# *Diana Bold*

This is a work of fiction. Names, characters, places, and incidents are products of the author's imagination or are used fictitiously and are not to be construed as real. Any resemblance to actual events, locales, organizations, or persons, living or dead, is entirely coincidental.

***Dark Promises***

By Diana Bold

Copyright May 2022

Cover Artist: Mandy Koehler Designs

Editor : Eve Paludan

# Dedication

F or Beth Hale. Thank you for the amazing brainstorming help! I couldn't have pulled this series off without you.

# Prologue

*London – December 1901*

L    "Where on earth are we supposed to sit?"

Lady Jocelyn Layton, the Countess of Aston, blinked in confusion at the huge circular table in front of her. Though set with sparkling crystal and china interwoven with garlands of greenery and flowers, the lovely presentation was missing one very important thing.

Her sister, Lady Evelyn Lindsay, grinned, her green eyes sparkling. "Oh, I love it! Allison is turning up her nose at old traditions. She married a commoner, so what better way to make him feel comfortable than to not have assigned seating arrangements based on rank?"

The sisters had just come from their friend Lady Allison Croft's wedding to Quinn O'Brien, a former police inspector. They were about to partake in the wedding breakfast that followed at the home of Allison's older brother, the Earl of Hawkesmere. Though Jocelyn loved Allison dearly and wished her all the best in her new life, the flouting of every social convention had her head spinning.

"How are the rest of us supposed to be comfortable, though?" Jocelyn asked her sister in a whisper. "There are no place cards!"

Evelyn just shook her head and laughed. "We can sit wherever we like! What freedom!"

Feeling very out of her element, Jocelyn sat rigidly in the seat just in front of her, and Evelyn took the chair to her right.

"I didn't spend my entire life learning the rules of society only to be put in situations where they are useless," Jocelyn groused.

"Our education should have been spent learning more than trivialities such as the proper fork to use," Evelyn replied. "I would have rather learned about philosophy and calculus than walked around balancing a book on my head!"

Evelyn was two years Jocelyn's senior and was a confirmed bluestocking at twenty-four. She spent her days campaigning as a suffragette. Jocelyn admired and loved her very much, except when she was ridiculing everything Jocelyn was good at, which was quite often.

Unlike her sister, Jocelyn had excelled at etiquette lessons, had a very successful debut, and married well. But her husband, Albert Layton, the Earl of Aston, had died two years after their marriage. That had given her the wealth and freedom to take Evelyn in when their parents had died in a carriage accident last year. But every once in a while, Jocelyn would have liked a little acknowledgment from Evelyn that her skills, too, had merit. They'd provided the roof over their heads, after all.

Allison and Mr. O'Brien entered the room then, laughing, their blond heads bent together as they shared a private joke, and all of Jocelyn's irritation fled. How could she care about something like a round table with no place cards when her friend had obviously met the man of her dreams and was gloriously happy?

"I still don't understand what she sees in him," Jocelyn whispered to her sister. "But I'm happy for her."

"How can you *not* see what she sees in him?" Evelyn whispered back. "He's handsome, intelligent, and kind. Any woman would be glad to have such a man."

Jocelyn sighed. She hadn't actually spent much time around Allison's new husband, but perhaps Evelyn was right. She'd never thought of herself as elitist, but it just seemed so wrong that Allison, who was the daughter of an earl, should take up with a man who was Irish, had spent a good portion of his life in an orphanage, and then worked with the dregs of society. The *ton* had turned their backs on Allison, and Jocelyn was quite aware that her own reputation was suffering for being here today. But she loved her friend dearly, and she'd rather have her reputation stained than have abandoned Allison on such a special day.

Before she could say anything else, a man drew out the chair to her left. She glanced up and realized that he was Mr. O'Brien's best man, a tall, lean man with dark hair and piercing blue eyes.

"May I join you?" he asked, lifting a dark brow.

She nodded stiffly, still a bit rattled by the unconventional seating arrangements. The wedding had been quite small, with only about thirty people in attendance. Jocelyn knew almost every person in the room except, of course, the man she was now going to have to sit next to. If the proper etiquette had been observed, she'd be close to the head of the table, nowhere near this man, who would be down at the foot.

A hint of bay rum teased her senses as he sat down, which was actually rather pleasant. She glanced surreptitiously at him from the corner of her eye, taking in his plain brown suit and slicked-back hair. He had a stiffness to him, a direct way of speaking, which made her think he'd once been a military man. She'd have to ask Allison.

Then she shook her head at herself, wondering why she cared. It wasn't as if she'd ever see him again after today.

"Sebastian Ness," he said, putting his napkin in his lap. "I am an inspector with the Metropolitan Police."

He obviously didn't know that someone else was supposed to formally introduce them. He certainly shouldn't be doing it himself. However, now she felt she had no choice but to reply.

"I am Lady Jocelyn Layton, the Countess of Aston. This is my sister, Lady Evelyn Lindsay," she replied tersely.

"That's a mouthful." He grinned, completely unaware of his *faux pas*. "Pleasure to meet you, ladies."

She found herself smiling wryly in return. Though she would never admit it to Evelyn, maybe this man would not be the worst dinner companion. He was certainly pleasant on the eyes.

"Are you the one who took over for Inspector O'Brien when he got hurt?" Evelyn asked, leaning toward Jocelyn so she could be part of the conversation.

In any other situation, Jocelyn would have been embarrassed by her sister's interruption, but Inspector Ness didn't seem to mind.

"I am. We were sorry to see him go, but he still consults with us sometimes, and he seems very happy in his new life." He gestured toward where Allison and Mr. O'Brien sat. "Lady Allison has been very good for him."

"And he for her," Evelyn said. "Allison's whole family seems to be lucky in love."

Jocelyn's gaze was drawn to Allison's three handsome brothers, who had filed into the room and were scattered around the table with their lovely brides. All of them did indeed seem to be glowingly happy, even though they'd been married for years. But every single one of them had also married far beneath them. Was that the trick? Was it impossible to marry among the *ton* and be happy?

Jocelyn's own marriage had been a disaster. At eighteen, she'd been married off to a man older than her father. He'd been cruel and condescending, and he'd died just months after the birth of their son, leaving her to raise his heir alone.

"Do you disagree?" Inspector Ness asked her, seeming to pick up on her discontent.

She stiffened even more if such a thing was were possible, embarrassed to have been so easy to read. "I do not. My sister is correct. Allison and her brothers all seem to have found love."

"But you don't believe in it for yourself," he surmised matter-of-factly.

"I don't know that I believe in it at all. Love, that is," she surprised herself by saying.

Evelyn gasped. "Jocelyn! How can you say such a thing? Of course, love exists."

"I don't know," Inspector Ness mused, catching Jocelyn's gaze and holding it. "I'm inclined to agree with the countess. Lots of people claim to have found it, but it never seems to last. I believe it's generally nothing more than lust and a sad desperation to have someone else to cling to."

Jocelyn knew she should be shocked by his coarse language, but she found she couldn't be upset with his message since it so closely mirrored her own views on the matter. "Exactly! I am perfectly happy with my own company. I don't need to pretend I'm in love to give my life meaning."

"Well," Evelyn said with a shake of her head. "I feel sorry for both of you. Neither of you will ever find true happiness if you go through life with that attitude."

Jocelyn laughed at her sister's words, but her gaze held Inspector Ness's for a long moment, feeling as though she'd finally met a kindred soul, even if their only similarity was in their goal to never be fooled into believing themselves in love.

# Chapter One

L*ondon – January 1902*
"Lady Aston?"

Jocelyn looked up from her morning tea to find Abbie Morton, her son Oliver's nanny, standing in the dining room doorway with a worried frown. "Yes, Abbie?"

Abbie shifted nervously, her dark eyes filled with concern. "I poked my head in Lady Evelyn's room on my way down... um, to say good morning... and she wasn't there. I checked with the upstairs maid, and Evelyn's bed wasn't slept in last night. I'm quite worried."

The friendship between her sister and the nanny didn't bother Jocelyn in the slightest, and she wished Abbie wouldn't be so hesitant to admit it even existed. Jocelyn knew very well that, most mornings, Evelyn and Abbie took breakfast together in the nursery.

"Did she say anything about going to a meeting last night?" Jocelyn asked with a frown. Evelyn was quite active in the women's suffrage movement, often putting herself in dangerous situations, even though Jocelyn had begged her to stop.

"No, my lady." Abbie shook her head, making tendrils of dark hair waft around her serious, elven face. "And she usually always does. I even go with her whenever my duties allow it."

Jocelyn nodded, her thoughts racing and a sense of foreboding settling deep within her. "Thank you for letting me know. Go back upstairs and check on Oliver, and I'll find out where Evelyn is."

Bending into a deep curtsey, Abbie left the room, though her worry lingered behind her.

*Oh, Evelyn. What have you gotten yourself into now?*

With a sigh, Jocelyn pushed to her feet and hurried up the stairs to her sister's room, hoping that somehow both Abbie and the maid had been wrong, but as purported, Evelyn's bed was still pristinely made, and her sister was nowhere to be found.

After questioning all of the upstairs servants, Jocelyn sent a footman to have her driver ready her carriage. She feared she knew where her sister might be. Unfortunately, this wasn't the first time Evelyn had been out all night. The last time it had happened, she'd been arrested and spent the night in jail.

A shiver went down Jocelyn's spine at the memory of her lovely, gently raised sister stuck in a filthy jail cell. Evelyn had been surrounded by all manner of cretins, who'd shocked her nearly to death with their crude comments. When Jocelyn had gone to bail her out, Evelyn had promised to never again put herself in such a situation, but Jocelyn should have known that wasn't a promise her sister could keep. Evelyn's passion for her cause was far greater than her fear for her own personal safety.

Still, Jocelyn couldn't shake the feeling that this time was different. Evelyn usually spoke about a big suffrage rally for weeks before it happened, and she hadn't said a word about attending a meeting in the last few days. She'd been a bit quiet at dinner last night, though.

As Jocelyn waited on the front steps for the carriage to be brought around, she tried to think where she should go to try and bail out Evelyn this time. Depending on where her sister had been arrested, she could be in any of London's local precinct houses, and Jocelyn knew Evelyn well enough to doubt it had happened in Mayfair.

*Inspector Sebastian Ness!*

The memory of the man she'd met at her best friend Allison's wedding last month suddenly came to her, and she decided the precinct he ran in Bethnal Green was as good a place to start as any.

Truth be told, he'd crossed her mind more than once since Allison's wedding. She hated to presume upon their brief acquaintance as their connection was tenuous, to say the least. Still, if he didn't have Evelyn in his jail, perhaps he could at least make some calls and point her in the right direction.

And it would give her an excuse to see him again.

INSPECTOR SEBASTIAN Ness was crossing the precinct lobby when the front door opened, and a lady breezed in with a gust of winter air. He froze, his gaze captured by her brilliant auburn hair. He swallowed dryly as he realized that she actually *was* a lady. Jocelyn Layton, the Countess of Aston. He'd met her at his friend Quinn O'Brien's wedding, and then, as now, he'd been captivated by her beauty.

*What the hell is she doing here?*

Whatever it was, it couldn't be good. A lady like her didn't venture down to a neighborhood like this unless something was dreadfully wrong.

One thing he knew for certain was that he didn't have time for this.

Since being promoted to inspector and taking over J Division, he'd had not only the day-to-day operations of the precinct to deal with but had also been tasked with catching a murderer they'd dubbed The Viper, who'd already butchered two young women. The last thing he needed was for an honest-to-God lady to heap more trouble his way.

With a sigh, he intercepted her before she could reach the desk sergeant. "Lady Aston. What can I do for you?"

She flushed, glancing around at the handful of people in the lobby with obvious embarrassment. "May I speak with you in private, Inspector?"

He nodded and led her down the hall to his office, carefully leaving the door open a crack for propriety's sake before taking a seat behind the desk and gesturing to the chair in front of it. She settled herself carefully, her gloved hands folded neatly in her lap, then lifted her beautiful green eyes to his.

"Inspector, may I ask... Is my sister Lady Evelyn Lindsay being held here?" Her cheeks were painfully red now, nearly the color of her flaming hair.

He frowned. "Held? What do you mean?"

"Was she arrested?" She dropped her gaze as though unable to hold his for another moment. "I only ask because she did not come home last night, and she's been known to protest for women's suffrage. She was arrested once before."

When he only stared at her, agape at the thought of holding a countess's sister in one of his cells, she cleared her throat and tried again.

"I'm terribly worried about her, and I'd like to bail her out and take her home, no matter what she's done."

He vaguely remembered a mousy blonde who'd been at her side during the wedding. A bluestocking, he'd been told. But he was still a bit flabbergasted at the thought of someone such as Lady Evelyn Lindsay being arrested. They did occasionally round up suffragettes, but he was fairly certain there had never been a lady among them. He hated to admit it, but if there had been, she probably would have been treated with kid gloves, not thrown into the holding cells with the rest.

"I'm sorry," he said, realizing he'd let his silence stretch far too long. "I'm afraid we don't have your sister in our custody."

She let out a sigh, but he couldn't be certain whether it was relief or despair. "I know I have no right to ask this of you; we hardly know each other. But is there a way you can find out if she's being held *somewhere*? I need to find her."

As he stared into her entreating eyes, something shifted deep within him. Until the moment she'd stepped into his office, he'd have sworn he couldn't be swayed by a lovely face, but he suddenly wanted to slay dragons for her. Or, at the very least, find her bluestocking sister.

"Of course," he said gruffly. "If you'll wait here for a moment, I'll have my sergeant telephone around and see what he can find out."

This time, there was no mistaking her relief. "Thank you so much, Inspector."

Nodding, he stood and exited his office, giving the sergeant his orders and then flagging down Constable Pond. "Will you find some tea and biscuits for the lady in my office?"

"Biscuits?" Pond asked, his eyes widening. "Tea, I can manage. But I don't think we have any biscuits."

"Go to the café across the street," Sebastian growled, tossing him a few coins.

"Yes, sir."

Feeling a fool, wondering why he cared whether Lady Aston had a biscuit, he marched back to his office. "My sergeant is working on it," he told her, resuming his seat. "And Constable Pond will be bringing you some tea and biscuits shortly."

She gave him a gentle smile, but he could tell she was still worried. "Thank you."

"Anything else I can get for you while we wait?" He couldn't help it. She just looked so lost and afraid that he wanted to make things better for her.

"No, thank you. You're doing more than enough already." She gave a small, embarrassed laugh. "I suppose you don't often have someone like me in here looking to bail someone out."

"No. In fact, I'm almost certain you're the first lady I've ever had in my office." He held her gaze. "Why did you come here instead of one of the other precincts?"

She flushed a bit again. "Well, I didn't know where to start. And you were very kind at the wedding breakfast. I thought you might be able to help."

Her words warmed him, even though he knew they shouldn't. She'd just admitted that she'd come here with the express purpose of presuming upon their acquaintance. But he was surprised that she'd remembered him at all. Women like her usually seemed to look right through him.

"Well, I hope that I can," he said truthfully. "Hopefully, we'll find out where your sister is, and then you can take her home."

"I know you must think I should put a stop to her suffrage activities," she said in a rush. "But it's easier said than done. She's a grown woman, and she's very passionate about her cause. Besides, I don't know that I'd stop her if I could."

Sebastian sat back in his chair, surprised that she was being so open with him. He hadn't asked her for any information, and he could only surmise that she was babbling in a fit of nerves and embarrassment.

"You're her sister, not her keeper," Sebastian reassured her. "I think it's admirable that you're here, willing to bail her out of whatever scrape she's gotten herself into. And I certainly don't fault her for wanting to fight for women's right to vote."

"You don't?" she asked, sounding surprised.

He laughed dryly. "Of course not. I've seen far too much injustice in the world. I commend anyone willing to combat that."

"You spent some time in the army, didn't you?" she mused.

He wouldn't have thought she'd know even that much. Had she asked their mutual friends about him? The thought pleased him for some reason.

"Six years," he answered, wishing he could forget that time of his life. "I've been with the police for six years now as well. And I'm not certain which line of work has shown me the most ugliness."

Her green eyes widened. "You must think me so very sheltered. I'm sorry to be taking up so much of your time for something like this. I'm certain you have more important things you could be doing."

Any misgivings he'd felt upon first seeing her had vanished as they'd continued to talk. This lovely young woman was truly worried about her sister. The other things he had to do today could wait for a while until he could ease her mind. If he could send her and her sister home safely, it would be a rare, good day, and he was badly in need of one of those.

"Nonsense," he said lightly. "I'm happy to be of help."

Pond knocked on the open door, then stepped in holding a battered tea service and a plate with several biscuits. The young man was flushed as though he'd been running, and Sebastian felt bad for sending him on such a ridiculous mission. He was sure Lady Aston wouldn't have cared if there were biscuits. Still, he felt glad that he could offer them to her.

"Thank you, Pond," he said, giving the young man a grateful smile.

Pond grinned back, then sketched an awkward bow in Lady Aston's direction. "My lady."

Once Pond had left, she gestured to the tea set. "Would you like me to pour?"

He nodded, feeling completely out of his element and wondering why he had ordered tea in the first place. A man like him was hardly suited to having tea with a lady.

He found himself mesmerized by her practiced and graceful movements as she went about the tasks that should be entirely mundane. She poured them both a cup of the steaming brew, then took one of the biscuits, making him feel ridiculously vindicated for having sent Pond out to get them.

They sat in silence for a few moments, but surprisingly, it wasn't awkward. He found himself far more comfortable with this woman than he should be.

At last, she set her cup down and met his gaze. "I know it sounds foolish, but I have a sinking feeling that something terrible has happened to Evelyn."

Her green eyes were a bit glassy, as though she was struggling to hold back tears, and he knew that she truly believed that her sister was in grave danger. As much as he doubted that someone like Lady Evelyn Lindsay was in any serious trouble, he knew she was desperate for someone to listen to her fears. "We'll find her," he assured her. "I'll help you."

The words came out sounding like far more of a vow than he'd meant them to, but he couldn't call them back now. He felt strangely committed, even though Lady Evelyn did not live in his jurisdiction and this wasn't his responsibility.

"Thank you." She managed a shaky smile. "I believe you will."

Before he could say anything else, Pond came back in, still looking a bit harried. "Sir? The sergeant told me to let you know he's called around, and Lady Evelyn Lindsay is not in any jail in London."

Lady Aston let out a small gasp, but Sebastian kept his focus on Pond. "Thank you, Pond. That will be all."

In his heart, Sebastian had been certain that they'd find Lady Evelyn in a cell somewhere, chagrined and frightened. But since they hadn't, Lady Aston's fears seemed a little harder to dismiss.

"Where could she be?" she asked, imploring him with those gorgeous eyes to give him an answer he didn't have.

"I don't know," he answered. "But let's go find her, shall we?"

# Chapter Two

Jocelyn allowed Inspector Ness to help her into her carriage, her mind awhirl with everything that had happened so far that morning. The bad feeling she'd had since she first found out her sister was missing had intensified with every passing moment, and now that she knew Evelyn had not been arrested at one of her suffrage protests, it had grown to a clamor of dread and worry.

Where on earth could Evelyn be? It wasn't like her to disappear without a word.

She settled into the forward-facing seat, and the inspector sat down across from her.

"I'm very grateful for your help," she told him nervously as the carriage jolted forward. He seemed a very busy man, and Mayfair wasn't even part of his jurisdiction, so she was surprised he was helping her at all.

"I could use the distraction," he answered, sounding weary. "I've been swamped with trying to find out who killed those girls from Mercy House, and I'm really not getting anywhere with it. Sometimes it's good to get out of my office and clear my head."

Jocelyn nodded sympathetically. She knew more about those horrific murders than most women of her station would, simply because Allison was the benefactor of Mercy House. Her friend had been living with her during the time that the murders had taken place, and Allison had told her all the salacious details, much to Jocelyn's dismay.

"Where are we going first?" she asked.

"I thought we'd go to your house. I'd like to look through Lady Evelyn's things, see if I can find any clues about where she might have gone."

Jocelyn felt a little twinge of guilt about letting a stranger poke through Evelyn's things, but what else was she to do? She hoped Evelyn would understand that she'd felt like she didn't have any choice but to let him try to find some answers. She supposed she should have looked a little more thoroughly before she'd dragged the inspector into this.

"Of course. Can you tell my coachman to head for home, then?"

He nodded and leaned out the window, yelling up at the coachman, then ducked back inside. "Tell me more about your sister," the inspector said, leaning comfortably back in his seat, stretching his long legs out before him, drawing her gaze to his muscular thighs encased in serviceable black trousers. "Maybe you'll say something that will help me figure out where we might best find her."

She met his bright blue gaze, trying to ignore the little thrill of attraction that ran through her. She'd been intrigued by him at the wedding, if only because he'd agreed with her that love was an illusion. But during the hour she'd spent at the station with him, she'd been unable to help but notice that he was an attractive man.

A very attractive man.

His hair was a deep, rich chestnut, thick and slightly wavy, though he kept it cut short. His eyes were a piercing blue, and he towered over her by nearly a foot. She also liked his demeanor. He was a bit gruff but exuded confidence and capability. She felt that if anyone could find Evelyn, it would be this man.

She sighed and tried to focus on the matter at hand. What details of Evelyn's life would be most important for the inspector to know?

"Evelyn's always been quiet and bookish," Jocelyn said at last. "She's two years older than me, which makes her twenty-four, but she's never married." She debated telling him why but ultimately decided against it. She didn't think that had anything to do with her sister's disappearance. "After our parents died last year, she moved in with me. We get along well, and she generally keeps me apprised of her comings and goings, though, of course, she doesn't have to."

"Does she often stay out all night?" he asked.

Jocelyn shook her head emphatically. "Only the one time I told you about when she was arrested. But even then, she managed to send word to me, letting me know what happened."

"You said that she is involved with the women's suffrage movement. I assume she has friends there. Is it possible they were out late, and she just decided to stay with one of them?"

She bit her lip. "I suppose. But I'm certain she would have called or sent word. She would have known I'd worry."

"What about gentleman friends?" he asked casually, as though what he was suggesting wasn't completely scandalous. "Is it possible she spent the night with one of them?"

"She has no gentlemen friends," Jocelyn assured him testily.

He didn't look as though he believed her, but thankfully, he let the matter drop. "Is there someone involved in her suffragette group we could talk to? Someone who could tell us if Lady Evelyn attended a meeting last night?"

Jocelyn bit her lip. "I'm sorry. I feel like I should know who Evelyn's friends are, but her cause has never held much interest to me, so I rarely pay attention when she talks about it." As she spoke, her shame and embarrassment grew. Evelyn's activities were important to her; Jocelyn should have listened. If she had, she wouldn't have had to enlist the inspector's help.

"Equal rights for women doesn't interest you?" he asked, raising a brow. "Voting? Property rights? I find that odd. Since you're a woman."

She frowned, stung. "It's not that I don't want that. I just don't believe I'll ever see it in my lifetime."

"Not if women like you, the ones who actually have some wealth and power, don't do anything to try and change it," he said evenly.

"I..." She didn't know what else to say because he was absolutely right. How was it that Evelyn had talked to her endlessly of this to no avail, and this man, who was little more than a stranger to her, had made her feel like she should do something with just a few careless words?

He smiled a bit. "You don't seem like the sort of woman who would want a man to make all your decisions for you. I know Allison certainly doesn't like that."

His familiar mention of her friend jarred her a bit, but again, he was right. "When my husband was alive, he didn't allow me any freedom at all. He told me where I could go, what I could wear, even what I could eat." Heat crept into her cheeks. "I know it's terrible to say, but when he died, I felt such freedom."

"I did not know you were a widow." His blue eyes were surprisingly gentle. "How long has it been?"

She swallowed, glad he hadn't voiced any judgment. She didn't think she'd ever admitted that to anyone before. Maybe not even herself. "Two years. He was much older than me. Sixty-five when we got married."

He nodded thoughtfully. "Then I doubt it was your choice to marry him. Don't you want your daughters and their daughters to be able to decide for themselves who they should wed?"

A laugh escaped her. "You sound like Allison. She refused to marry for anything less than love, and now that she thinks she's found it, I can't say she was wrong."

She didn't think it was necessary to tell him he was right about it not having been her choice to marry Aston. He'd been right far too many times in their conversation, and that was something she wasn't used to. Most of the men she knew were seldom right about anything.

"Quinn and Allison are very lucky to have found each other," he said, surprising her once again with this hint of sentimentality. At first glance, she never would have guessed that he had a romantic bent. He seemed far more likely to break heads than hearts.

"Yes," she agreed. "I had my doubts at first. I was afraid Allison had ruined herself beyond repair socially by marrying Quinn, but anyone who sees them together can tell that she made the right choice."

She hadn't expected to be having such a strange conversation with this man but realized that perhaps he was just trying to take her mind off Evelyn. Warmth and gratitude filled her. It seemed she'd made the right choice as well by going to him about this matter.

Before she could find the words to express how much it meant to her that he'd been so helpful, they pulled up in front of her house. "We're here," she told him, hoping he could find something in Evelyn's bedroom that would give them the answers they needed to find her.

SEBASTIAN ALIGHTED from Lady Aston's carriage and then blinked up at the towering townhouse with the white marble façade. Well, her elderly husband had certainly left her well provided for. This monstrosity of a house could have comfortably billeted his whole company.

Smiling grimly, he turned back around to help Lady Aston down as well, asking himself as he did so why the hell he was here. This wasn't any of his business and not his responsibility. He should be back at his desk, proving to Assistant Commissioner Blackstone that he was worthy of the trust he'd placed in him by promoting him to inspector.

But as Lady Aston's small yet voluptuous body slid down his, and he gazed down into her troubled green eyes, he knew why he was here, even if it made no sense at all. This tiny, auburn-haired sprite was perhaps the loveliest thing he'd ever seen. From the moment she'd walked into his station this morning, he'd been unable to take his eyes off her.

"Thank you," she whispered breathlessly as she stepped

away from him, and to his surprise, she seemed just as affected by the chemistry between them as he. A shaft of rare winter sunlight caught the fiery strands of red in her auburn hair, and he wanted nothing more than to press against her once more and kiss her senseless.

"You're welcome," he murmured, turning back toward the house, trying to calm his own racing heart. His attraction toward her was completely inappropriate and not at all conducive to conducting this investigation.

By the time the butler opened the front door and they stepped into the warmth of the front entryway, he'd successfully managed to tamp down his ardor. Thanks to years of dealing with high-stress situations, he felt he was once again in the right frame of mind to figure out what had happened to Lady Evelyn.

The interior of Lady Aston's home was every bit as elegant and ostentatious as the outside. They entered a grand two-story hall, crowned by a ceiling graced with a breathtaking mural of angels in a cloudy sky. He tried not to show how out of place he felt as a footman came over to take their coats.

"Thank you, Thomas," she said to the young man. "Did Lady Evelyn return while I was out?"

Thomas shook his head. "I'm sorry, my lady. She did not."

Lady Aston's face fell, and she turned back to Sebastian. "I'd offer you tea, but since we just had some, do you mind if we go straight to Evelyn's room? I'm anxious to see what you can find."

"Of course," he murmured. "Lead the way."

They climbed a curving staircase toward the next floor and then walked down a long hallway carpeted in deep burgundy.

Along the way, they passed countless paintings and sculptures, any one of which probably cost more than he earned in a year. The vast inequality between the average man and those who lived in Mayfair had never been so clear to him.

At last, Lady Evelyn stopped before a door on the left side of the hall and turned to look at him. "I feel a bit guilty about invading her privacy this way. About letting a stranger go through her things."

"We don't have to do this if you don't want to," he told her, understanding her concern, though it would certainly make things easier if they could find something to point them in the right direction.

Warring emotions flickered across her face, but she suddenly nodded and pushed open the door. "She'll just have to forgive me. If she'd sent word to me so that I wouldn't be worried, this wouldn't be necessary."

He smiled at her rationalization and followed her inside. He liked her pragmatic nature. He'd always thought that the ends justified the means.

Lady Evelyn's room was actually a bit more spartan than the rest of the house had been. Though the room was large and well-appointed, the pale-peach color of the walls and drapes was very subdued. One whole wall was covered in bookcases, which held hundreds if not thousands of leather-bound books. A cozy, well-worn chair sat in front of the marble fireplace, the bed was against the wall near the door, and a desk stood on the other side of the room.

"She's very tidy," he mused, walking over to look at some of the titles on the bookcase. He'd expected them all to be about women's suffrage, but her tastes were far more eclectic than that, covering a wide array of nonfiction and a healthy section of fiction as well. "And well-read."

Lady Aston nodded. "My sister nearly always has her nose in a book."

He ran his fingertips along the leather spines, looking for something out of place, somewhere she might hide things.

Nothing jumped out at him, but he would pull them all out individually if need be. However, Lady Evelyn hadn't seemed like someone who kept dark secrets. Also, this room fairly shouted safety and security. She probably wouldn't feel the need to hide anything. She had no reason to believe someone would be looking through her things.

He wandered toward the desk, pleased to see a diary sitting right on top. He picked it up. "Do you mind if I look through this?"

Lady Aston bit her lip. "Go ahead. But don't tell me what you read unless it's relevant."

He nodded and leafed through the most-recent pages of neat, beautifully penned entries until he got to the one from yesterday.

*M wants me to meet him in the park. What could he possibly want after all this time? The whole thing is rather mysterious, and I'm still contemplating whether I should go.*

"She was going to meet someone she calls 'M' in the park," he said, lifting his gaze to Lady Aston's concerned green eyes. "Do you have any idea who she was talking about?"

She shook her head. "M? I have no idea. Are you certain it's a man?"

Instead of answering, he showed her the entry. She read it and then looked up at him with a puzzled frown. "It could be nearly anyone. I can think of a dozen men we're acquainted with who have that initial in either their first or last names. And which park?"

"I would appreciate it if you'd make a list of everyone you can think of," he told her, skimming through the entries from the last month. None of them mentioned anything about a man named 'M." Though she often referenced someone she was obviously in love with, someone she referred to as "A." She also talked about her sister, "J," and someone else, "O," though it was all fairly inane. It was exactly what he'd expect to find in the diary of a bored socialite who dabbled in the women's suffrage movement.

Finally, he placed the diary back down on the desk. "Is there any park, in particular, she liked to frequent? Where would be the first place you'd look if she told you she was going to the park?"

She bit her bottom lip, and he forced his gaze away from the lush sight, reminding himself once again to focus on the task at hand and not his lovely companion.

"She does like to go to Postman's Park to read. It's within walking distance, and she didn't take one of our carriages, so either she walked, took a hired hack, or someone picked her up," she said at last, having obviously thought about her answer.

He liked that. Too often, people answered him without truly thinking about it.

"Let's go speak to whoever was working near the door and see if anyone saw her leave. They might be able to provide us with an answer to that. If we don't find anything to point us in a different direction, we can walk to the park ourselves, talk to people along the way, and see if any of them saw anything."

Relief washed across her lovely features. "Yes, that sounds like a good plan."

# Chapter Three

As Jocelyn walked toward Postman's Park with Inspector Ness at her side, her fear and sense of dread grew. Their inquiries of the butler and the footmen who'd been working in the front of the house last night had yielded nothing. Evelyn had left on foot about 5:30. She hadn't told anyone where she was headed.

She wasn't quite certain what Inspector Ness hoped to find at the park, though she couldn't question his logic in searching there. She just didn't understand why her sister would have met someone there, then not have come home all night.

Evelyn certainly wouldn't still be in the park nearly twenty-four hours later.

And who was "M?"

"This is a nice walk," Inspector Ness said stiffly, obviously trying to make small talk to put her at ease, though he didn't seem the type to think much of talking just for talking's sake.

She gave him a grateful glance, struck once again by the sharp contrast of his sky-blue eyes against his thick, black lashes. "Yes, I think my sister comes here several times a week."

"What about you?" he asked. "Don't you ever walk to the park to read?"

She shook her head. "When I have time to read, I prefer to

do so in the comfort of my home. Evelyn has always been more outdoorsy than I am. This red hair and pale skin of mine tend to make me fry like an egg in the sun."

He smiled a bit at that but didn't comment.

Heat crept up her cheeks at that needlessly intimate detail. Why had she said that? He could probably tell just by looking at her that she had not been made for bright sunlight.

They walked in silence for a while after that, but it didn't seem awkward. He strode beside her, a large, comforting presence, and for perhaps the first time in her life, she felt truly safe. She had no doubt that no one would approach or accost her with him at her side.

But it was more than just his physical size and power. Those gorgeous eyes of his were full of wisdom and inner strength as well. She'd reached out to him today simply because she'd known no one else who could help, but as the day progressed, she'd begun to think she couldn't possibly have picked anyone more suited to her quest to find Evelyn.

Still mulling this strange feeling over in her head, she realized they'd passed the huge General Post Office building and reached the park's perimeter. "Here we are," she told him unnecessarily. "What are you hoping to find?"

He stopped and looked around, taking in the entire area. "I'm not sure," he said with a shrug. "I suppose I'll know it when I see it."

Unsatisfied with his response, she looked around herself. She'd been here before, of course, though she didn't frequent it as often as her sister did. The park was a lovely place with an abundance of trees and flowers, though it was surrounded by tall homes and buildings, making it seem a bit smaller than it actually was. A large wooden loggia with a tile roof housed the Memorial to Heroic Self-Sacrifice, which had only recently been completed to honor ordinary people who'd died to save someone else, and a small stone building that looked to be some sort of groundskeeper's cottage.

"Did you know they dug up two cemeteries to make room for this park?" she asked him, shivering a bit at the thought of it. "I've always found that a little disturbing. All those bodies moved elsewhere in the name of progress. I hope their souls were able to find peace, but I can't help but feel this place must be a bit haunted."

"There's nothing to fear from the dead," he told her, and in his eyes, she saw that he'd experienced more than his share of death. "It's the living you need to be concerned about."

She wondered if he'd been forced to kill during his time in the service. He might have had to as a policeman as well.

"I know," she murmured, feeling foolish. "It just seems that some of those souls, buried here for years, might have lingered."

"If you believe in ghosts, you have to realize that in a city as old as this one, they must be everywhere, not just this park." Though his words were a bit teasing, she didn't think he was making fun of her, just pointing out a truth.

She sighed. "I know. I just don't want my sister to join them."

He reached over and squeezed her hand in reassurance, then suddenly became all business. "Let's split up," he suggested. "We can cover more ground that way. Just look for anything that might belong to Evelyn and ask anyone you come across if they've seen her. Look for anything that seems out of place."

She nodded, realizing he must do this all the time, but her hand still tingled a bit from his touch, even through her glove. It was rare for the people she knew to touch each other for any reason, but she appreciated his attempt to offer comfort.

What she did not appreciate as much, however, was his casual attitude about the whole thing. She found it frustrating, but only because her sister meant so much to her. Other than her son, Evelyn was the only family she had left. She couldn't bear it if anything had happened to her.

He headed to their left, and she went right, crisscrossing across the paths and flowerbeds as she kept her eyes out for something that could help her find her sister. She only came across a few people, and none of them had seen anyone resembling Evelyn, although none of them had been here yesterday either.

Occasionally, she'd look across the park to see Inspector Ness meticulously searching his section, and the sight of him kept the rising panic at bay. She had no doubt if there was anything to be found, he would find it.

She lingered in front of the memorial, reading the plaques of some of the people who'd already been honored, saddened by the case of Alice Ayres, a servant who'd run into a burning house three times to save her employer's children, only to be overcome by smoke herself. She wondered if Abbie would do the same for Oliver and hoped they never had to find out.

Nearly an hour passed before she finally met Ness back where they'd started. Her feet were killing her. She should have changed into walking shoes when she'd had the chance. The February chill had also cut through her until she was chilled to the bone. Exhausted, she looked at him hopefully. "Did you find anything?"

He shook his head, killing her hope. "No, but the gardener's shed is locked, so I'm going to have to find who has the keys and ask if we can search it. How about you?"

"Nothing," she said on a sigh.

He checked his timepiece, then glanced around the park once more, as though Evelyn would suddenly step out from behind a tree and call, "Boo!" Then he met Jocelyn's worried gaze. "Let's return to your house. If Lady Evelyn comes home, you won't know if we're out combing the city for her. If she does show up, please send word to me immediately. Until I hear otherwise, I'll still be taking steps to find her."

"What sort of steps?" she asked, falling in beside him as they headed out of the park.

"Well, Mayfair is not my jurisdiction, so first, I need to pay the boys at Scotland Yard a visit and apprise them of what's going on. They can send a few of the lads out to search the other nearby parks and get ahold of the caretaker of this one to open the shed. I'll check the hospitals to make sure she didn't have an accident. If you make me a list of the people your sister might have been referring to in her journal and also any friends who might know where she went last night, I'll send some of my men to start questioning them."

Jocelyn bit her lip, knowing that once she authorized this, Evelyn's reputation would be ruined. No matter where she'd been last night, people always tended to think the worst of an unmarried woman. Would Evelyn ever forgive her if there ended up being a plausible explanation?

"You don't have to do this. It hasn't even been a full day since you last saw her," Ness said, as though he'd read her mind.

"You can just go home and wait for her to return. It's very likely that she is off somewhere with a friend or lover. If she still hasn't come home by tomorrow morning, we can start the search for her again."

Neither of those possibilities seemed remotely plausible to her. If Evelyn were going to stay the night with a friend, she would have sent word. It wasn't in her sister's nature to worry her so needlessly. And as for a lover... No, she was certain Evelyn hadn't spent the night with her lover. She wished the inspector would quit insinuating that but supposed he was used to dealing with a different class of people.

Squaring her shoulders, Jocelyn made her choice. "I know it sounds mad, but I am certain that something terrible has happened to her." Tears stung her eyes, the bad feeling in the pit of her stomach growing stronger. "I'd like to start the search now."

He stopped and gazed down at her, his handsome face unreadable, but his blue eyes filled with such warmth and understanding it took her breath away. "I believe in gut feelings. In my experience, they are nearly never wrong. If you feel this strongly that something bad has happened, I'll do whatever I can to try and find her before it's too late."

She couldn't remember a time when a man had so easily taken her at her word. And she didn't even have anything solid to go on, just this feeling that something wasn't right. It endeared him to her in a way she couldn't express.

"Thank you," she whispered. "That means everything."

He nodded, his cheeks coloring ever so slightly as he started moving purposely once again toward her home. She rushed to keep up with him, her short legs having to take two steps for every one of his. She realized how much he'd been matching his pace to hers before, but now he seemed on a mission. His swift decisiveness comforted her, and so she didn't mind that she was practically running by the time they reached her front steps.

"If you'll come in with me for a few moments, I'll write down those names," she told him breathlessly.

He smiled as he suddenly realized his swift strides had been too much for her. "You should have told me to slow down."

She shook her head. "I'm glad you're in a hurry." Her voice wobbled, even though she was trying hard to be brave. "I fear that there is not a moment to spare."

Taking a deep breath, she led him back inside, straight to the study, where she grabbed a pen and started writing the list of Evelyn's friends and men they knew with the initial M that she'd been compiling in her head on their walk back. After scribbling for several moments, she lifted her gaze and sighed. "I've written down quite a few, but I'm so frazzled I'm certain I'm forgetting some."

He leaned over her shoulder and skimmed the page. "This should do for now. Keep thinking about it and write down the rest as they come to you. I'll come back at the end of the day and collect them from you, plus tell you anything I've learned."

She'd been standing in front of the desk writing, and now she was pressed between the cool wood of the desk and the heat of his big body. He wasn't touching her, but she could feel him behind her, his breath tickling the nape of her neck as he spoke. A shiver of awareness traveled through her, and though it was completely ill-timed and unwarranted, she couldn't help but be surprised and intrigued.

Was this desire? She'd certainly never felt anything even remotely like it before. Cataloging the sensation away to take out and examine later, she turned, but he hadn't moved. She found herself staring up at him, his handsome face looming above her, so close she could see the faint dark stubble of new beard that had somehow cropped up during their time together.

He cleared his throat, and her gaze followed the movement.

"Thank you," she whispered, feeling oddly light-headed. "You didn't have to do all of this for me, didn't have to take me seriously at all, and I really appreciate it."

His gaze drifted to her mouth, then jerked back up to meet hers. "Strolling through a lovely park with a beautiful lady has hardly been a hardship."

*He thinks I'm beautiful.* It was an absurd thought, given everything else that was going on, but it gave her a little thrill anyway. All of Allison's erotic feelings for Mr. O'Brien suddenly made a bit more sense.

Acting on pure instinct, she lifted up on her tiptoes, placing her arms around his neck and pressing her lips gently against his cheek. Never in her life had she been moved to do such a thing, but his skin was so warm beneath her lips, his scent so masculine that she simply wanted to breathe him in for a time.

He stiffened at first but then put his arms around her as well, hugging her tight for an endless moment. "I'll find your sister," he promised, his voice a mere breath of sound in her ear.

She looked up at him, her heart thundering in her chest, her gaze centered on the beautiful contours of his mouth. A soft sound of yearning escaped her despite her best attempts to hold it in. She'd never in her life been kissed for the sheer pleasure of it, and she suddenly wanted to be. Very badly.

As though he'd somehow heard her silent pleas, or perhaps because he felt this attraction between them as well, he suddenly leaned down and captured her mouth with his own. His lips were warm and soft, and he tasted of tea and sugar. She pressed more fully against him as the kiss went on, as they learned each other in such an intimate way, their lips and tongues dancing together.

"Mama, who is that man?" The tiny voice broke through the haze of desire and tenderness that enveloped her, jerking her back to reality. She dropped her arms and stepped away, looking toward the doorway where her three-year-old son stood with the nanny, Abbie.

"So sorry, my lady," Abbie said in a rush, obviously mortified. "He saw you come in and insisted on coming to find you."

"It's all right, Abbie." Ignoring her flaming cheeks, Jocelyn bent down and opened her arms, catching Oliver as he flung himself against her. Standing, she turned back to Inspector Ness. "May I introduce my son, the Earl of Aston? Oliver, this is Inspector Ness. He is trying to help me find Aunt Evelyn."

The little boy looked at the inspector with wide, searching eyes. She wasn't even certain if he knew what a policeman was. "Is she under the desk?"

Inspector Ness barked out a laugh, looking quite flustered himself. "Nice to meet you, young man." He nodded at the women. "I should be on my way. I'll let you know if I hear anything."

She watched him leave, her pulse still racing. As worried as she was about Evelyn, she couldn't be sorry she'd kissed him or stop the wish that she hoped she could do it again soon.

# Chapter Four

S ebastian hailed a hack outside the countess's townhouse, still a bit flustered by the way Lady Aston's soft lips had felt against his, the passion she'd stirred in him, and the even more alarming fact that she was the mother of a young son who would one day take the reins of a vast estate. He didn't know why the fact shocked him so. The first thing an old aristocratic man with a beautiful young bride would do was get an heir in her.

But he'd started to think in directions he had no right to, and the boy's mere existence stopped those thoughts cold.

Sebastian had been raised by a widowed mother. He'd seen her parade a stream of lovers through her bed, each worse than the last. But she'd become completely enamored with each one, thinking he would be the one to change their circumstances, that he'd marry her and pull them out of the poverty they'd sunk to. Her eternal quest to do so had left her very little time or energy to spend on her young son.

He'd always promised himself that he'd never become involved with a woman with a child. And this child... this child was a bloody earl.

He scoffed at himself as the hack turned toward Scotland Yard. What a fool he was, to pretend like he was the one who would have decided whether Lady Aston would have become his lover. Just because Quinn O'Brien had managed to marry a lady didn't mean that a woman like Lady Jocelyn Layton would ever want a relationship with someone like him.

Although she was a widow and could discreetly take a lover if she chose to do so, she'd made it perfectly clear that she did not believe in love, and a woman like her, a lady, would never dally with a man with only the intention of a physical release.

He should never have kissed her. Not only had it been highly unprofessional, but he'd also been so swept away in the moment that he hadn't even checked if the door was locked. As a result, they'd been caught by both her son and the nanny. He could only hope the woman was discreet, and that seeing his mother kissing a stranger hadn't scarred the child for life.

With a sigh, he turned his thoughts back to the matter at hand. Lady Aston had probably allowed his kiss not because she was attracted to him in any way but because he was helping her find her sister. And as the day had worn on, he'd become less convinced that Lady Evelyn had simply run off with some man and hadn't bothered to let her sister know.

She'd most likely met someone at that park, and it seemed more and more certain that the meeting hadn't gone as planned.

His mind drifted from Lady Evelyn to the killer he'd been hunting for months. Once again, he felt a spurt of guilt for having abandoned his search for the day, but perhaps this was exactly what he'd needed to clear his mind and help him look at things in a new light. This was a reminder that terrible things happened all over the city, not just his little corner of it.

Ten minutes later, he was walking through the hallowed

halls of Scotland Yard in the Norman Shaw building on the Victoria Embankment, nodding to people he knew as he made his way toward his supervisor's office. The original building on Whitehall Place had a rear entrance on a street called Great Scotland Yard, and that had become the public entrance. Over time, the street and the police headquarters had become synonymous. Although the building had moved, the name, which was originally derived from the street name, had remained.

He squared his shoulders outside the door, always a bit intimidated by Mandrake Blackstone's pedigree, though he tried to never let it show. It had been that way in the army too—always a man born to the aristocracy who gave the orders. He should be used to it by now.

He knocked lightly, hoping that Blackstone had time to see him.

"Come in," Blackstone called, sounding annoyed.

Sebastian entered Blackstone's immaculate office, which had forest-green walls and carpet and heavy walnut furniture, and found his supervisor at his huge desk, bent over a stack of papers with a look of grim concentration. However, his face cleared when he saw Sebastian standing there.

"Inspector Ness," he said, sounding surprised. He had inky-black hair, dark piercing eyes, aristocratic features, and a tall, broad frame. Sebastian thought the man was a few years younger than himself, his family name having helped him jump the ranks, but nothing in his bearing made him seem too young for his position. "Did we have a meeting today?"

Sebastian shook his head as Blackstone gestured to an empty chair in front of his desk. "I've come to ask for help on a matter that came my way this morning. I've done what I could, but it really isn't my jurisdiction."

"If it isn't your jurisdiction, then why are you bothering with whatever it is?" Blackstone snapped. "Don't you still have a killer on the loose?"

Sebastian decided to ignore that. Blackstone was frustrated. They all were. "Lady Jocelyn Layton showed up at my precinct this morning, wanting to know if I was holding her sister in one of my cells," he answered instead. "She's very upset, said that her sister, Lady Evelyn, did not come home last night. Lady Evelyn is active in the women's suffrage movement, and Lady Aston thought she might have been arrested. I had my sergeant call around, and that does not appear to be the case."

Blackstone pushed his stack of papers away and leaned back in his chair. "I know the ladies well. I have since we were children. I wonder why she didn't come to me."

Sebastian wondered that as well. Why ask for help from a lowly inspector when she knew the assistant commissioner? His heart gave a strange thump at the thought that perhaps she'd been looking for a reason to see him again.

"I helped her search her sister's room, and we found a diary entry that said she was meeting someone named 'M' at Postman's Park yesterday afternoon. We then searched the park, but we didn't find any sign of her. However, I am inclined to believe that something did happen to Lady Evelyn. From everything Lady Aston told me, her sister doesn't seem the type not to come home or at least send word."

"I agree," Blackstone said, his sudden tension palpable. "Lady Evelyn is a very sensible woman. She would not like to cause the countess to worry."

"There was a locked gardener's shed that I couldn't access, but we searched the park pretty thoroughly. I wonder if you could have someone try to find the keys to that and also mobilize some more men to aid in the search? I'm afraid I don't know the area well enough to be of much help."

"Of course." Blackstone ran his fingers through his black hair, leaving it standing on end, his dark eyes troubled. "The last thing we need is a missing lady."

"Let me know if you find her," Sebastian said, pushing to his feet.

Blackstone nodded. "Of course."

AFTER INSPECTOR NESS left, Jocelyn paced the sitting room, feeling as though she'd go mad from frustration and worry. She knew he'd been right to say that she should stay home and wait for Evelyn's return, but as the hours passed with still no sign of her, her dread that something horrible had happened grew.

And then there was the kiss! She still couldn't believe that he'd kissed her. That she'd *wanted* him to kiss her! She'd initiated the intimacy between them with the kiss of gratitude she'd placed on his cheek, so what was he supposed to think?

She pressed her fingertips to her lips and sank into a chair in front of the fireplace, getting lost for a moment in the memory of the moment they'd shared.

That kiss had certainly not been anything like her husband's!

The earl had not really seen the need to bother with kissing her very often, and she'd been glad of it. His teeth had been rotten, his breath rancid with alcohol and cigars. The few times he'd pressed his mouth to hers had been very unpleasant. She'd had to fight not to gag and pull away.

But Inspector Ness... *Sebastian*... His kiss had been a pure joy. He'd made her finally see that perhaps what had happened between her and her husband had been an aberration. What had her father been thinking, to marry her to someone that old?

*He was thinking that an earl like himself was the best I could possibly do. He wanted his grandson to have a title and a fortune of his own.*

She glanced over at her son, who was sleeping peacefully on the sofa. She could never regret her marriage because it had given her Oliver. But nothing she was currently in possession of was truly hers. When Oliver grew up, she'd be at his mercy, the way she'd been at the mercy of her father and then her husband.

It had been a miracle that her husband had left her as Oliver's guardian, instead of naming some man to do it instead. She could very easily have gone from the control of one man straight to the control of another. But Albert had hated his younger brother, had been certain that if Matthew were to get ahold of Oliver's inheritance while he was a child, he'd spend it before her son reached his majority. So he'd stipulated that Jocelyn and a retinue of solicitors were to be in charge until Oliver became a man.

Her husband's death had granted her more freedom than nearly any woman she knew.

Still, if she was being honest, she had to admit that none of this had been what she wanted. She'd cried for days after her father had told her what he'd planned.

Abbie entered the room, her gaze on her sleeping charge. "Would you like me to take him up to the nursery, my lady?"

"No, let him sleep here," Jocelyn said softly. "He's helping to take my mind off things."

The nanny cleared her throat. "Have you heard anything from Lady Evelyn?"

Jocelyn shook her head. "No, I'm afraid not."

Abbie held out a scrap of paper. "There's a meeting tonight. Here's the address. I don't think she'll be there, but maybe someone there might know something?"

"Oh, thank you!" Jocelyn took the piece of paper gratefully. "The inspector is supposed to come back later. Maybe he'll go with me."

"They won't like a man there, but maybe when they hear that Evelyn's gone missing, they'll allow it," Abbie said, shifting nervously. "I just don't know what could have happened! This is so unlike her!"

"I know," Jocelyn murmured, somewhat relieved that there was someone else who understood that her sister would never needlessly cause them worry. It had now been almost twenty-four hours since Evelyn had left the house. If she'd been able to send word, she certainly would have.

The thought that something was preventing her from doing so seemed more and more likely.

Abbie sighed. "If you don't mind, I'd like permission to go out looking for her this afternoon. I just can't sit here and do nothing. I'm going out of my mind with worry."

"Of course," Jocelyn told her. "Just try and be back by six or so. I'd like to go to the meeting with Inspector Ness."

"I will, ma'am. Thank you." Abbie left quickly, and Jocelyn

prayed that her sister's friend had better luck than she'd had.

WHEN SEBASTIAN RETURNED to tell Lady Aston that he still hadn't found her sister, he was surprised to find her waiting on the front steps of her townhome. Before he could even disembark from the hired hack, she strode up to meet him, her lovely face set in determined lines.

"My sister's friend told me there is a meeting tonight at this address." She thrust a scrap of paper toward him. "I'd like to go and see if she's there or if anyone there might know where she is. Will you accompany me?"

He'd planned to head home after speaking to her, but how could he possibly refuse the entreaty in those green eyes? Especially when he'd been unable to dig up a single thing that would help him find Lady Evelyn himself.

"Certainly." Jumping down from the hack, he handed the paper to the driver along with instructions to take them there, then handed her inside, settling across from her. He wondered if she'd ever ridden in a hired hack in her entire pampered life, but if it bothered her, she gave no indication.

"This day has been interminable," she muttered, as the hack jolted into motion. She looked absolutely exhausted. "Evelyn's friend, Abbie Morton, my son's nanny who you briefly met, went out searching for her for a while. I was hopeful that she might discover something, but she returned about half an hour ago without finding a trace of her. I am losing my mind with worry. I couldn't stay there any longer."

"Well, I spoke to your friend Blackstone at Scotland Yard," he tried to soothe her. "There should be a small army of constables out looking for her now."

"Oh! I forgot that Drake was the assistant police commissioner," she said, her eyes widening.

He wasn't certain if she was upset that she hadn't thought of going to Blackstone first, and he didn't like the familiar way she used Blackstone's first name. Was that... jealousy?

He scoffed inwardly at himself. He'd always thought jealousy a wasted emotion and couldn't believe he'd be so foolish as to feel it now. Even though she had kissed him so passionately earlier in the day, she had been born to be the wife of someone like Blackstone, not the mistress of someone like Sebastian. Irritated at himself, he tried to get his mind off the kiss they'd shared and focus on the matter at hand.

"In any event, I'm certain we'll get to the bottom of this soon." *One way or another.* Though he didn't say it, the words hung heavily between them. He'd been so certain in the beginning that her sister would drift in sometime during the day with some sort of story about where she'd been and what she'd been doing. The fact that she hadn't, that nightfall was upon them once again, seemed to be a harbinger of bad news.

Jocelyn obviously felt it, too. She sat so rigidly it seemed that she was ready to snap in half. Her obvious need of comfort, and the thought that for once in his life he might be able to provide it, struck him to the core.

Damning propriety, he swung over to the forward-facing seat beside her, putting his arm around her and drawing her against him. She went even more rigid for a moment, but then sagged against his side, pressing her face against his chest.

"Thank you," she whispered, her voice muffled against his tweed coat. "I know we shouldn't be doing this, but I'm so afraid that something has happened to her."

"I know." He stroked his hand lightly across her silken hair, marveling at how the setting sun highlighted strands of fire amid the varied strands of brown. She seemed so small and fragile in his arms, though he knew that wasn't entirely true. For such a little thing, she had a will of iron.

"Do you think someone there will be able to help us?" she asked.

"I hope so," he answered. "If these women are good friends of hers, they might know something. Maybe she told one of them where she was going. It can't hurt to ask."

She snuggled a little more fully against him, and the passion that had flared between them earlier was there again, simmering under the surface. For a long while, he simply held her as the hack bounced along the increasingly potholed streets. To his surprise, he found that he was getting comfort from their embrace as well. It had been so long since anyone needed him this way.

For the first time in a long time, his thoughts drifted to his wife, who'd died nearly a decade ago. Hell, he wasn't certain if Marina had *ever* needed him this way. His wife had been lovely and spoiled, the only daughter of a wealthy businessman. She'd liked the idea of being married to a soldier and had loved him in his bright red uniform. They'd had a whirlwind romance that had ended with their marriage and a few passionate nights where he'd begun to suspect that she'd not been a virgin. However, the moment he'd shipped out, her attention had fallen elsewhere. She hadn't been made to be a soldier's wife, waiting patiently alone for months at a time. She needed to constantly be the center of attention, and when he hadn't been there to give that to her, she'd found someone who could.

"My husband never held me or offered me comfort," she said softly, surprising him with her candor. "He had little use for me once he'd secured my dowry and gotten me with child. There are times when I've felt sorry for Evelyn, knowing she'll never have children or a husband of her own, but then I remember what it was like to be married to the earl and know that perhaps she is the lucky one."

"I'm sorry your marriage was like that," he replied, squeezing her shoulders gently in a one-armed hug. "You deserved more than that."

She laughed breathlessly. "I didn't really think that there *was* more. I thought all marriages were like mine. But now that I see Allison with her inspector and have gotten to know her brothers' wives, I'm starting to think that perhaps some people do manage to find peace and comfort together."

He thought about telling her of his own marriage, the hopes he'd had going in, the soul-crushing disappointment when he'd found out Marina had run off with someone else while he'd been out of the country, but now did not seem the time.

Before he could think of anything to say, she gave a self-conscious laugh and eased a bit away. "Listen to me. A man gives me the slightest kindness, and I'm waxing poetic about marriage after I completely denounced it the first time we met. You must think me a fool."

"It's perfectly fine to change your mind about things when presented with a different view of them. But I don't think marriage was what you were denouncing that day. It was love," he reminded her, very aware that the two were entirely different things.

She shrugged prettily. "Well, I have no experience with love at all."

Silence fell between them once again, but this time, she reached out to him, twining her fingers with his and holding his hand tightly. Her hands were slim and lovely, encased in silken white gloves, a stark contrast to his large, calloused, bare paws.

It seemed a travesty to him that no man had ever loved this smart, beautiful woman. She was definitely worthy of such emotion, though he stood by his previous statement that what people called love was most likely a mix of lust and loneliness. He'd thought he'd loved Marina, but in the end, after her betrayal, it had been fairly easy to walk away. His supposed love had turned into bitterness and disdain, and he'd never entered into such emotions with any of the lovers he'd had since.

He stole another glance at the woman beside him, the long line of her graceful throat, and something clenched deep inside him. Not love... certainly not that. But... something. Attraction, definitely. And he actually *liked* her. She was easy to talk to, and he'd found that, for him at least, women rarely were. But it was more than that. From the first time he'd sat down next to her at that wedding breakfast, there'd been some sort of connection between them, a recognition that somewhere deep inside, they were the same.

Did she feel it, too? As his gaze fell once again on their clasped hands, it certainly felt as though she might.

But he wasn't an idiot. They'd been thrown together by extraordinary circumstances, and once the matter of her sister was resolved, she'd have no need for a lowly police inspector.

Before his thoughts could go any farther down that path, the hack pulled up in front of a nondescript row of brick storefronts. Number 217 bore a sign out front that read *Rose's Apothecary*.

"This must be it," Jocelyn said, a hint of nervousness in her voice.

A lot seemed to be riding on the next few minutes as far as her sister's fate was concerned. They might go inside and find Evelyn was simply a bad sister, that she'd gotten caught up in her own life and hadn't realized that Jocelyn was worried. Then again, they might find out that none of these women who probably knew Evelyn well had any idea where she was, which would put them back to square one. Worse, it would make it even more likely that something terrible had happened to the young woman in question.

He squeezed her hand tightly, meeting her gaze. "No matter what they say, we won't give up, all right? We will find her."

She gave him a poor attempt at a smile. "Thank you. For everything. I know you didn't have to do any of this. I appreciate it more than you know. I don't know how I would have survived today without you."

"You're stronger than you think you are," he told her softly, hoping that she'd never have to truly find out. He forced a smile "All right, then. Let's go to our first women's suffrage meeting."

# Chapter Five

Jocelyn let Sebastian help her down from the hired hack, grateful for his solid presence beside her. He exuded strength and authority, and she had no doubt he'd know exactly what to do and say once they went inside.

Rose's Apothecary was in a neighborhood that seemed neither bad nor especially good. She would have been nervous about having to come here alone, yet Evelyn had apparently come here alone all the time. It made her extremely uncomfortable that her sister had a whole side that Jocelyn had never really gotten to know.

Once they found her sister safe and sound, Jocelyn promised herself she'd take more of an interest in Evelyn's good works. Sebastian had been right. How could change ever come about if women like her, those who held a bit of power, wealth, and influence, didn't do anything? After her husband's death, she'd attained a level of freedom most women could only dream of, yet what had she done with it? She was starting to realize that she'd put herself in as much of a box as Albert had.

Sebastian reached the door and opened it for her, setting off a little bell that tinkled merrily as they entered. To her surprise, it seemed just an ordinary apothecary shop, bottles of pills and potions lining the crowded shelves, a bored-looking female clerk behind the long counter at the back of the store. No rabble-rousing female protestors to be found.

Jocelyn exchanged a worried look with Sebastian. Had they come to the wrong place?

"May I help you?" the clerk asked.

Sebastian stepped forward. "Yes, I'm Inspector Ness from the Metropolitan Police, and this is Lady Aston. We're here for the women's suffrage meeting. Lady Aston's sister, Lady Evelyn Lindsay, is one of your members, and she's been missing for a full day. We know she was supposed to come here tonight, and we're hoping that she did or that we can talk to someone who might know where she's disappeared to."

"Evelyn is missing?" The woman's entire demeanor changed. "I'm Rose Grantham. Evelyn is one of my closest friends. I would hate it if anything had happened to her. Please, tell me what I can do to help."

Relieved that this woman seemed inclined to help them, Jocelyn gave her a strained smile. "She didn't come home last night, and I haven't heard from her since. I'm certain you know how unlike her that is."

"I was wondering why she hadn't shown up tonight. You're right. It's very unlike her not to be the first to arrive." Biting her lip, the woman opened a door behind her. "The rest of the girls are in the back having tea. I was just about to close up the shop and join them. This way, please."

Sebastian and Jocelyn followed Rose through the door and past a maze of boxes until they reached a storeroom in the back of the building that had been converted into a meeting room of sorts. A circle of about a dozen chairs sat in the middle of the room, but only seven of them were full. Everyone looked up as they entered, several of their gazes locking unwelcomingly on Sebastian.

Jocelyn was somewhat surprised to see Allison's lady's maid, Heather Fields, was one of the attendees, though she supposed she shouldn't be. When Allison and Heather had lived with Jocelyn and Evelyn, her sister and Heather had become great friends. Evelyn had never let someone's station in life determine whether she should be friends with them. Jocelyn was starting to realize how often she had judged people based on their pedigree, and she vowed never to do so again.

Rose cleared her throat. "This is Inspector Ness and Evelyn's sister, Lady Aston. They are looking for Evelyn. Apparently, she's gone missing."

The women all started talking at once, their distress at having a man invade their meeting wiped away by their obvious concern for Evelyn. As Sebastian began answering their questions and asking some of his own, Jocelyn's heart sank. It didn't seem as though any of them knew where Evelyn might be, and she had no idea where else they could look.

Just when she thought all hope was lost, Heather drew her a little off to the side. She was a lovely woman with dark hair and wide blue eyes. "I last saw Evelyn two days ago. We met for coffee and to discuss the agenda for tonight's meeting. She seemed a little distracted."

"Did she say why?" Jocelyn asked eagerly. "Did she tell you anything at all that might help us find her?"

Heather bit her lip, then nodded. "She mentioned that a man had been sending her notes. Though she'd turned him down in the past, he'd decided that she must reconsider. She thought it was funny at first, that any men would become so fixated on a spinster like herself, but he'd grown more and more persistent. She said she'd finally agreed to meet with him that evening to tell him she was not going to change her mind and ask him to stop contacting her."

"Did she mention his name?" This had to be the mysterious M, but she still wasn't certain who it could be. As far as she knew, Evelyn had never had any serious suitors.

Heather shook her head, looking upset. "No, I don't think she ever mentioned him by name, and if she did, I can't remember it."

"What did she do with the notes?" Jocelyn asked. Perhaps, if she could find them, she could figure out the identity of the man sending them.

Heather frowned. "I am assuming that they went right into the fireplace. She was quite undone by them. I cannot see her keeping them for any reason."

Jocelyn unease grew. "Did anything she said make you think she would have changed her mind once she talk to him, that she might have willingly gone somewhere with him without sending word to anyone about where they'd gone?"

"No." Heather shook her head emphatically. "She seemed upset by the entire situation."

Why hadn't Evelyn told her any of this? Tears stung Jocelyn's eyes, and she blinked rapidly, trying to hold them at bay. It wouldn't help Evelyn at all if she were to utterly break down. She needed to remain as strong as Sebastian thought she was until they got to the bottom of this.

But then she promised herself she would have a good long cry about it all.

"Thank you, Heather," she said, offering the woman a shaky

smile. "Please let me know if you remember anything else. You're welcome to come by anytime."

"I will," Heather replied. "I do hope you find her. She's the rock of this group. Any of us would do anything for her."

"I should have come with her," Jocelyn said, feeling more guilty with each passing moment. "She asked me a dozen times, but I never made the time for it."

"Well, we'd be happy to have you," Heather assured her. "I've been trying to convince Allison to come as well. We could really use women like the two of you. A few members of the *ton* could make all the difference in the world."

They stood silently side by side for about ten more minutes while Sebastian finished questioning the other women, but nothing any of them said seemed very helpful. Heather had probably provided the best information, and unfortunately, it didn't really tell them much they didn't know.

At last, they took their leave, and Jocelyn told Sebastian what she'd learned as soon as the hack jerked into motion.

"Do you have any idea who this man might be?" Sebastian asked her when she finished.

"No, I'm afraid not. Heather didn't know his name, and she thinks Evelyn burned the notes, which actually sounds true to form. She didn't keep many personal papers." She shook her head, entirely at a loss. "I don't understand it. Why didn't Evelyn tell me about these notes? Why didn't she talk it over with me at all?" She still didn't understand it. She'd thought that her sister shared everything with her.

"Maybe she didn't want to worry you," Sebastian reasoned. Then he sighed. "Don't beat yourself up over that. There could be a hundred reasons, and most of them probably don't have anything to do with you. But at least now we have some sort of path to follow. Good job getting this information."

Her cheeks heated at his praise. Especially since she sensed he didn't give it out often.

"What do we do now?" she asked, shivering a bit. The sun had gone down while they'd been in the apothecary, and now it was bitterly cold, the faint scent of snow in the air.

"Now, we get you home," Sebastian told her, putting his arm around her and drawing her close once again. "You're shivering, and there's nothing else we can do tonight. Don't forget that there are men out looking for her as we speak. Someone might turn up something tonight. If not, we'll pick it up again in the morning."

She sighed and pressed against him, wondering how he could still feel so warm. She'd never imagined it would feel so very right and wonderful to be in a man's arms, and the kiss they'd shared this morning came rushing back to her. Far better to think about that than the fact that they were no closer to finding Evelyn than they'd been when they'd sat out together this morning.

Here, in the semi-privacy of the hired hack, she could let herself accept the comfort this man seemed so willing to give to her. She pressed her face against the scratchy tweed of his suit vest, simply breathing him in. Dear Lord, he smelled fantastic, bay rum and something else, something she could only describe as Sebastian. Far better than any of the perfumed dandies she'd ever known before.

Soon, she began to warm up, not just because of his heat but because a spark of her own had ignited deep within her. Something about this man made her realize that perhaps she did have some passion within her. Maybe she did have some of those mysterious needs that others spoke of.

She lifted her gaze to his, stunned by her daring. "Would you kiss me again?"

A passing lamppost threw a slice of light into the hack and caught in his bright blue eyes. "I know you're upset. Are you sure this is what you want?"

"It's the only thing I'm certain of right now." She pressed her mouth to his, uncaring if this was right or wrong. Her entire world had been turned upside down today, and this man seemed to be the only thing anchoring her in place.

He stiffened for just a moment, then groaned softly and kissed her back, wrapping her tightly in his arms, chasing the last of the chill away. She sank into his kiss, letting all the fear and stress of the day melt away into pure pleasure.

She'd never imagined that it could be this consuming, this beautiful. The whole world fell away, and it was just the two of them, drowning in heat and desire.

Suddenly, the hack pulled to a stop, and the driver rapped on the roof. She pulled away and looked out the window to see that they were back in front of her house. She felt dazed, as though she'd been ripped out of a wonderful dream.

"We're here," she said unnecessarily, hoping that no one had caught her in her indiscretion. But the night provided a protection of its own; she could barely see Sebastian in the dark interior of the hack. Besides, who on earth would believe that the Countess of Aston had been kissing a police inspector in a hired hack on the streets of Mayfair?

"We are." He smiled and then gave her one last lingering kiss. "Keep your chin up. I'll speak to Blackstone in the morning and then come by and let you know if there's any news."

"Thank you," she told him, wondering why she didn't feel more awkward with him, given the intimacies they'd shared.

He got out and handed her down, squeezing her gloved hand before releasing her. "Until tomorrow then."

She nodded and gave him one last lingering glance before turning and walking up the stairs to her house.

Her butler opened the door before she reached it, and she gave him a grateful smile. "Thank you, Winston. Has there been any word from my sister?"

"I'm afraid not, my lady."

With a heavy sigh, Jocelyn nodded and let him help her with her coat. "I'll be in my room if there's any news."

"Very good, my lady."

Once she'd shut her bedroom door behind her, she sagged against it, feeling exhausted and overwhelmed. This had been one of the most upsetting and confusing days of her life. Her worry for her sister was crippling, but the moments she'd shared with Sebastian had been unlike anything she'd ever experienced before.

She prayed that Evelyn came home soon so that she could further explore these exciting and amazing feelings.

# Chapter Six

T he next morning, as soon as Jocelyn was dressed, she raced down to Evelyn's room, throwing open the door and hoping against hope that either the whole thing had been a terrible nightmare or that her sister had somehow returned during the night. But Evelyn's bed was still pristinely made, the room silent and dark, the curtains still drawn against the dawn.

*Oh, Evelyn. Where are you?*

How was this happening? How could her staid, boring sister have just vanished without a trace?

Backing slowly out of the door, she headed upstairs to the nursery, nodding tiredly at Abbie as she picked up her little blond-haired son and hugged him tightly.

"Any word?" Abbie asked, but she sounded as though she already knew the answer to that.

"No. Inspector Ness and I went to the meeting, but none of them knew anything about where Evelyn might be."

Abbie scrubbed her hand across her face. "I went everywhere I could think of that she might be yesterday. I just don't know what could have happened."

"Something bad," Jocelyn said, giving voice to her worst fears. "If she could have come home, she would have."

"I feel the same way," Abbie said. "I'm so worried about

her."

They shared a long, poignant moment, bonding over their shared love for Evelyn. Jocelyn didn't think anyone else in the world knew her sister the way the two of them did. If something had happened, Abbie would be the only one who could understand how much the world had lost.

Frightened of the direction her thoughts were going, Jocelyn tried to head them off. "I think I will just stay up here with the two of you today. I need to be with Oliver."

He smiled up at her. "Mommy will stay."

"Yes, baby. Mommy will stay." She tried to summon a smile for her adorable little son.

For the next two hours, she played with Oliver, letting his youthful exuberance completely consume her, trying to put all thoughts of Evelyn from her mind. She'd fallen so deeply into the world of toy soldiers that she jumped when the butler cleared his throat in the doorway.

"My lady, Inspector Ness is here to see you."

She exchanged quick, worried glances with Abbie, then pushed to her feet. "Thank you, Winston."

She rushed down the stairs to the drawing room, slowing down only when she reached the closed doorway. She stopped for a moment and took a few deep breaths, then finally opened the door.

Sebastian had been standing in front of the window, staring down at the street below, but when she entered, he turned, and their gazes caught and held, heat flaring between them. Would it always be like this? Or if she was to give into it, would it quickly fade? That thought had kept her up last night. That, and her worry about Evelyn, of course.

The thought of her sister was like a bucket of cold water poured over her head, and she remembered in a rush that the attraction between them was not the reason he was here.

"Is there any news of my sister?" she asked, hurrying toward him.

Sebastian shook his head regretfully. "No, I'm afraid not. I've just come from Scotland Yard, and though they still have dozens of men out searching, they haven't found any sign of her. Likewise, no hospitals reported having her as a patient."

She sank down into the nearest chair, trying to stay strong even though she wanted desperately to have the cry she'd promised herself. But she wouldn't, not until her sister had been found. She had to stay strong and keep her wits about her. She stared down at the tips of shoes, just visible beneath her dark-green skirts. "That's not bad news though. As long as they haven't found her yet, there's still a chance that they will." She didn't know who she was trying to convince—him or herself.

She peeked up at Sebastian, and the unguarded look she caught on his face told her everything she needed to know. He didn't think that Evelyn was going to be found.

Not alive, anyway.

She pushed to her feet, refusing to believe the resignation on his face. "We have to look harder. There has to be something we haven't thought of yet. Some clue we've missed."

Sebastian said nothing. He simply crossed to her side and wrapped her in a tight embrace, holding her quietly as she struggled not to give in to her threatening tears.

"Some investigations take longer than others," he said at last. "We've covered all the obvious places, so now we have to go back to the drawing board and follow leads that are not so apparent."

"Like that mysterious unwelcome suitor."

"Yes. But we won't give up. I promise you that."

She nodded against his chest, believing him. He didn't seem the type to give up on things, and she was grateful for that, even though her sister's disappearance made her more worried and frustrated than she'd ever been, which said a lot, given how she'd spent the years of her marriage.

His hands traveled up her back to her shoulders, and she almost groaned when his strong fingers kneaded the muscles there. "Poor thing," he murmured in her ear. "You're so tense, darling."

Her heart thrilled a bit at the endearment, and she wrapped her own arms around his waist, holding on tight. No one had ever called her darling before. "I'm so worried."

"I know you are," he said, and she could hear his own frustration leaking through his voice. "I'd do anything to take your worry away, to solve this for you."

That's what he was, she realized. A problem solver. He spent his whole life solving other people's problems. She wondered suddenly if anyone had ever done the same for him. Then she realized that despite the strange intimacy that had flared between them during the last few days, she knew next to nothing about this man.

His hands continued to knead the muscles in her shoulders, then moved on to her neck and upper back. The fanciful thought crossed her mind that he was somehow rebuilding her, making her his own.

"That feels wonderful," she admitted. "You never cease to amaze me. Do you give everyone you work with such service?"

His hands froze for a minute, then continued. "You know I don't," he chided. "You're special to me. I can't explain it, but you know it's true."

She did know it, and she suddenly felt bad for having said what she had, for trying to force these words from him. But she was feeling so lost, so confused by the emotions he pulled from her, that she'd desperately needed to know that he felt it, too. That he didn't seduce every woman who came to him with her problems.

Because that's what he was doing. Sebastian Ness was seducing her with his kindness, competence, and intelligence. She hated the reason that had thrown them together, but she couldn't be sorry that she'd gotten to know him.

"You're special to me, too, Inspector," she whispered.

"I would be honored if you called me Sebastian instead of Inspector. Especially since we're alone."

"Sebastian." His name rolled off her tongue so beautifully, and she liked the way it sounded on her lips.

"I'd be honored if you called me Jocelyn."

"Jocelyn." He said her name in a whisper, like a prayer.

The use of each other's names seemed to signify something. She just wasn't certain what that was.

She finally dared to look up at him, and the moment their eyes met, he kissed her again, this time with shattering thoroughness. She felt as though the times leading up to this had just been practice runs, and this was the main event. His hands came up to cup her face, feathering softly over her skin as though he was learning every feature, as though he wanted to imprint this moment across his mind for all eternity.

They kissed as though they had forever to do so, as though

terrible, frightening things weren't happening just outside that door. As though her sister would walk in at any moment and chide her for being so indiscreet.

At last, he broke away, staring down at her with such intensity it took her breath away. "I want to make you feel good," he whispered hoarsely. "Do you trust me, Jocelyn?"

She wasn't certain what he was asking, but she realized the answer was yes. Her answer to anything this man asked of her would always be yes. Even though she hardly knew him, she instinctively trusted him as she'd trusted no man before him, not even her father.

"I trust you, Sebastian," she breathed, and his eyes flared with something she hesitated to put a name to.

Stepping slightly away, he took her hand and led her to the sofa. Once she'd sat, he sank to his knees in front of her. The different in their heights was such that his face was still almost even with hers. To her shock, he put a hand on each of her knees and eased them apart so that his body was now pressed against the edge of the sofa between her thighs.

"Have you ever... either with your husband or at your own hands... had a sexual release?" he asked hoarsely.

Her eyes widened, shock filling her even as his words caused a persistent ache at the apex of her thighs. "No," she squeaked. "I don't even know exactly what you mean."

Surely you weren't allowed to touch yourself in such a manner? She'd never even considered such a thing. She'd been told since birth that it would be a sin.

He leaned forward and kissed her again, so tenderly it took her breath away. Then he pressed his forehead against hers. "I'd like to touch you in a way that will make you feel so good,

Jocelyn. I promise that it will make all of this go away, at least for a little while. Will you let me give that to you?"

She could only nod, afraid to ask what he meant, afraid to even think about it. But she did crave the escape he offered. She needed a few moments of respite from this clawing worry.

Still pressing his forehead to hers, he slipped his hands under her skirts, running his palms along the lace of her stockings and then the bare skin of her thighs. She gasped, biting her lip as the ache between her thighs grew until it was almost painful.

"You're so soft here," he breathed. "I love touching you this way."

Catching her mouth with his again, he kissed her deeply as his fingertips brushed against her most intimate spot. Though on some level, she'd known that was where this was headed, it still shocked her, immediately bringing back the memories of the way her husband had hurt her.

But Sebastian's touch was tender, gentle, a careful exploration as he learned what she liked and what made her shy away. "It's all right," he whispered between kisses. "Just relax."

"Something's wrong," she told him fretfully. "Am I... bleeding?"

He shook his head, his gaze tender. "No, darling. Nothing's wrong. This moisture is your body's way of preparing you for making love. It's supposed to be this way when you're enjoying it."

"Ohhhh," she said, embarrassment rushing through her as she realized how little she knew her own body.

Then he found a spot that made entire brain seem to shut down, indeed giving her the escape she'd wanted. His every touch there was exquisite, and she found herself straining against him, wanting more, reaching for something she couldn't even name.

As he continued to stroke that sensitive spot with his thumb, he gently inserted his forefinger inside her, and the combined sensation was more than she could bear. Her entire body contracted, waves of indescribable pleasure racing through her until she sank against the back of the couch, her legs still spread, her skirts lifted wantonly, feeling more at peace than she perhaps ever had in her life.

Slowly, he eased his hands out from under her skirts, then went about straightening them, at last leaning forward and wrapping his arms around her waist. "How do you feel?"

She sighed and buried her hands in his hair, idling twirling the dark strands around her fingertips. "I never knew it could be like that."

"That's a shame." He looked up at her, those blue eyes so earnest it took her breath away. "You deserve to be loved this way, Jocelyn. That bastard you were married to should have taken his time. Made it good for you."

A bitter laugh escaped her. "He didn't care if it was good for me. He didn't care about me past my ability to give him an heir." Suddenly, she frowned. "You didn't get any pleasure from this at all, did you? You didn't... find your own release?"

He smiled and eased away. "I loved every minute of it. And finding my own release was not what this was about. As I said before, I just wanted to give you a little escape from the heavy thoughts weighing you down right now."

His words did little to ease her. She wasn't comfortable with being strictly on the receiving end of things. "But... I feel like I should do the same for you."

He gave her a quick, passionate kiss, then pushed to his feet. "Some other time, perhaps? I'm really hoping this is just the beginning. Besides, I need to get back to work. I've stayed with you far longer than I should have when I have to find your missing sister." He stood there for a moment, looking down at her with an unreadable expression on his handsome face. "I don't think you have any idea how beautiful you are, Jocelyn. But I hope you'll give me the chance to show you."

His words lingered in her mind for a long time after he exited the room, and she couldn't stop the satisfied, infatuated smile on her lips.

*I have a lover.*

She'd never thought she'd say those words, not even to herself. She'd certainly never thought any man could make her feel the way he just had. If he could make her feel that good with just his fingertips, while they were fully dressed in her drawing room, she couldn't even imagine what other pleasures he might show her. And she suddenly had a fierce desire to learn how to make him feel that good in return.

*Allison would know...*

Part of her wanted to leap to her feet, order a carriage, and go directly to her friend's house to talk about all the conflicting emotions she was feeling, but immediately on the heels of that came the realization that Evelyn was still missing. How could she allow herself to feel this good about anything until her sister was found?

Even though it was seeming more and more likely that she never would be.

# Chapter Seven

After leaving Jocelyn, Sebastian hailed a hack to take him back to his station. As much as he wanted to devote all his time to looking for Evelyn, he had many responsibilities of his own, and he had to admit that he'd done all he could think to do. Evelyn Lindsay seemed to have disappeared into thin air, and he had to content himself with the fact that Blackstone had a small army of men out looking for her.

As he rode back across the city, he shifted uncomfortably in his seat, thinking of Jocelyn coming undone at his hands. She'd been so lovely, so responsive.

What he wouldn't do to have her in his bed for a whole night, just the two of them, without the specter of her missing sister standing between them. He wanted so much to be the one to show her how much pleasure could be had in lovemaking, especially since her introduction to it had apparently been so horrible.

But he knew he'd already crossed the line. She had far too much on her mind to be taking on any sort of affair with him. And he hadn't thought even once of her son this morning, of his promise to himself not to get involved with the mother of a young child. How had things gotten out of hand so quickly? He'd never been tempted so badly in his life. Somehow, he needed to find the strength to keep things between them professional, at least until her sister was found safe and sound.

He hated to think of the other alternative, what he'd do if Evelyn had met with some terrible end. If the worst happened, Jocelyn might never want to explore things between them further, and he wouldn't blame her.

Later that afternoon, he was attacking his pile of paperwork when Constable Pond stuck his head in his office. "There's a call for you, sir. Assistant Commissioner Blackstone."

A shiver of foreboding went through Sebastian. He couldn't have said exactly why, but he'd long ago realized that in his line of work, it was best to trust your gut instinct. Right now, his gut was telling him that Blackstone was about to deliver some very bad news. He pushed to his feet grimly and followed Pond down the hall to where the office telephone was kept.

The contraption still didn't make much sense to him, but since it had been installed, it had helped communication between precincts immensely. He held the receiver up to his ear. "Ness here," he said loudly, always feeling as though he had to practically shout.

"Ness, I need you to meet me at Postman's Park right away," Blackstone replied, his tone heavy with anger and sadness. "We've found Lady Evelyn in the gardener's shed." A long pause hung heavy on the line. "It appears she's The Viper's third victim."

THIRTY MINUTES LATER, Sebastian was back at Postman's Park, elbowing his way through the crowd of people who had gathered around the gardener's shed. A dozen or more constables were keeping back the onlookers, and several other inspectors and Blackstone stood near the door. When Blackstone saw Sebastian, he motioned for one of the constables to let him through.

"Are you certain it's her?" Sebastian asked, hoping against hope that it wasn't. "Are you certain it's Lady Evelyn Lindsay?"

Blackstone nodded grimly. "I've known Evelyn since we were children. I would recognize her anywhere."

Sebastian sighed, feeling as though he'd somehow horribly failed Jocelyn, even though odds were Evelyn had been dead before Jocelyn had even come to see him yesterday morning. All the way over here, he'd prayed that Blackstone was wrong, but the man would know his childhood friend. No escaping that the worst had happened. "Can I have a look?"

"Of course. I was hoping you'd get here before the coroner took her away. It appears to me that this is The Viper's doing, but since you've seen his work before, I'd like your opinion on the matter." Blackstone waved an arm toward the shed.

Sebastian entered the small space, which was filled with different gardening tools and implements. The heavy smell of soil in the air was tainted by the unmistakable scent of spilled blood. He slowly let his gaze fall to the floor, where a naked woman was splayed upon the dirt, her throat cut and gaping, her green eyes staring sightlessly at the ceiling.

He swallowed. No matter how many times he saw death, it never got any easier. He had a quick flashback to the morning of O'Brien's wedding when Lady Evelyn Lindsay had sat two chairs down from him, alive and inquisitive. She'd been intelligent, a crusader for women's suffrage, but now she'd never get to help all of those she might have.

Jocelyn would be destroyed by this.

Shaking away the thought, the suddenly personal aspect of this case, he forced himself to concentrate, to take in everything he could before they took Lady Evelyn Lindsay's broken body away.

All the way over, he'd wondered why Blackstone was so convinced this was The Viper's work—he'd been certain it couldn't possibly be—but staring at Evelyn now, he was inclined to agree. Her throat had been cut, and there were unspeakable wounds to her body. He only hoped that she had been dead when those other wounds had been inflicted. At her feet, there was a piece of paper with a single word, *whore*, written across it in red ink.

This was somewhat different, because with the other women, the word had been written on naked photographs they'd posed for to make money. However, it seemed very doubtful that Evelyn had ever had any such photographs taken of her own free will, so the killer wouldn't have had such a thing available to him.

But if not, if Evelyn had been what she seemed—a kind, responsible spinster—then why had she been targeted at all? Why would The Viper write this about her?

This departure from The Viper's normal sort of victim had to be a clue, it had to give some inkling of who the monster might be, but he'd be damned if he could figure it out. None of this made any sense.

He spent a few more minutes viewing the body from every possible angle and scanning the shed in hopes of finding some personal item The Viper might have left behind. They'd gotten lucky when the man had left his snuffbox behind at the first murder, but he seemed to have learned his lesson, because he didn't appear to have left anything behind when he'd done this.

Weary and saddened, he finally went to join Blackstone back outside. "I think you're right. It must be The Viper, but I have no idea why he'd pick someone like Lady Evelyn."

Blackstone ran his hand through his black hair in frustration. "The city was baying for our heads when it was prostitutes in Bethnal Green. Can you imagine the uproar when it gets out that The Viper murdered a lady in Postman's Park?"

Sebastian frowned, hating the fact that Blackstone was right. The murder of a lady was going to bring tremendous pressure on them. "It has to be him. We never leaked the information about the word *whore* being left at the scenes."

"He came here with the intention to murder her in this building," Blackstone said, pointing to a lock that lay on the ground, obviously cut open with some sort of a tool instead of opened with a key. "When we finally contacted the gardener, he showed up with the key, but it didn't work. He told us this was not the lock that belonged to this building. So the bastard must have cut the original one off himself and brought a new one with him."

"Do you suspect the gardener?" Sebastian asked.

"Not at all. He's been sick in bed for a week, foot infection, and had a nurse attending him the entire time. He'd just gotten back to work today."

Casting a quick glance around at the many houses and buildings that lined the surrounding streets, Sebastian nodded. "The Viper, whoever he is, must be familiar with this park then.

Perhaps he lives or works nearby. And the lock might help us. It looks expensive." The Viper could be watching them right now from any of the dozens of windows that looked over the park.

"I'll have someone look into the lock," Blackstone said tightly. "In the meantime, I don't know how I'm going to tell Lady Aston."

"May I do it, sir?" Sebastian asked. He couldn't stand the thought of not being there when she heard the terrible news. "I've been working with her for the past two days, and I promised I'd let her know the minute we found out anything."

"If you're sure you want to," Blackstone agreed, looking relieved. "Go and let her know and then meet me at Scotland Yard when you're done. I'll have the coroner work on Lady Evelyn's body right away, even if it takes him all night. We need to find out everything we can."

"I'll be there as soon as I can," Sebastian assured him, then walked quickly back through the crowd in the direction of Jocelyn's house, wondering why he'd taken this upon himself. He could easily have let Blackstone handle it. Their families were old friends, and she probably would have taken the news better from him anyway.

But they'd formed a bond, shared some poignant, intimate moments, and he'd been so committed to helping her find her sister. He felt it was his duty to tell her and also to be there to comfort her when she heard the news.

Night had fallen while he'd been investigating the shed. A bitterly cold breeze blew down the street, and he remembered what Jocelyn had said about ghosts haunting this place. Another gust hit him, and he fancifully imagined it was the ghost of Evelyn Lindsay, tearing at his hair and clothes with her icy need for vengeance.

*I will find out who did this to you. I swear I will.*

# Chapter Eight

Putting Oliver to bed while Evelyn was still missing had upset both Jocelyn and her son. He was used to his aunt being there, and Jocelyn didn't know what to say when he repeatedly asked where Evelyn was. He'd obviously picked up on the anxiety that both his mother and nanny were feeling, and he'd been a little bear all evening.

He finally cried himself to sleep, and she sat upon his bed for a long time afterward, trying to get her own racing emotions under control when all she really wanted to do was curl up next to her son and cry herself to sleep as well.

*Where are you, Evelyn?* She didn't know if it was a prayer or a plea, but the thought had gone through her mind at least a thousand times in the last two days.

She would love to believe her sister was out there somewhere, that some ridiculous set of misadventures had left her stranded but unharmed. However, deep in her heart, she knew that it was foolish to keep hoping that things would turn out that way. Evelyn would never worry her this way. *Never.* It always came back to that. If there was any possible way that her sister could have contacted her, she would have.

Pushing away such disturbing thoughts, she went to her own set of rooms, closing the door and leaning heavily against it as she stared blindly around at the little oasis done in rich purples and blues she'd built for herself during the first weeks of her marriage. This had always been her safe place, and she'd demanded that her husband not visit her here. Instead, she'd instructed him to send for her when he wanted her, and she'd gone to his rooms to perform her wifely duties. It had been the only bit of power that she'd ever managed to wrest for herself during those early days.

No bad memories haunted her here, but if Evelyn was gone... if something bad had happened to her... would she ever feel safe anywhere?

With a sigh, she forced herself to the bathroom, where she ran a hot bath. She disrobed without calling for her maid and gratefully sank into it, placing a glass of red wine on the rim of the tub. The heat of the water calmed her somewhat, and as she drank her wine, her thoughts drifted to the time she'd spent with Sebastian Ness.

A shiver went through her as she remembered the way she'd brazenly kissed his beard-stubbled cheek and then fallen so dangerously into his arms. Was this what attraction and desire felt like? Since she had no prior experience with either one, she wasn't really certain, but he made her feel things she'd never felt before. She wished that Evelyn hadn't gone missing, that she'd gotten to know Sebastian better at Allison's wedding when everything had still been right in her world and she could have entertained the idea of taking a lover...

She blinked, stunned that such a thought had crossed her mind. Reaching for her wine, she took another drink, but the thought had taken root and didn't seem to want to go away.

Why shouldn't she think such things? As a widow, she

could do whatever she wanted, as long as she was discreet. She'd just never wanted to before. She'd never dreamed she might want to do the things her husband had forced upon her ever again.

But suddenly, she couldn't stop thinking of the dreamy look on Allison's face when she'd described making love with Inspector O'Brien. She certainly seemed to enjoy it. No, she more than enjoyed it. She'd risked everything to be with the man who'd awakened desire in her.

Jocelyn thought of the way Sebastian had touched her, the glorious release she'd found at his hands, and also what he'd said about finding her own pleasure. Did she dare try such a thing here in the privacy of her bath?

Biting her lip, Jocelyn slowly ran her fingertips over her breasts, which were aching and pebbled, wanting to once more feel the incredible sensations she'd felt in Sebastian's arms this afternoon.

It felt wonderful, though heat flared in her cheeks and shame burned through her.

A sudden knock at the door made her gasp and drop her hands. "Who is it?" she called, expecting it to be the butler.

"It's Inspector Ness," he answered, then cleared his throat. "Sorry, my lady. I know it's late, but your butler showed me up. You said you wanted to know as soon as I knew something, and well... I know something."

She surged to her feet, reaching for her towel and looking around wildly, wondering what she should do. It would take forever to have Janette come up and make her presentable, but she couldn't possibly allow him in her room when she was fresh from her bath. Stepping out of the tub, she toweled herself off frantically, knowing from the tone of his voice that there was no time to waste.

"My lady?" he asked again, and she realized she hadn't answered him.

"Just a minute," she cried, reaching for her heavy velvet robe and wrapping it securely about her still damp body, belting it tightly at the waist. She glanced at herself in her vanity mirror, horrified to see her wild red curls frizzing crazily around her flushed face, her voluptuous curves easily discernible beneath the robe, but it couldn't be helped. She had to know what he'd found out. Besides, given the liberties she'd already allowed him, it would be ridiculous to worry about things such as modesty now.

He knew something about Evelyn, and she had to know what it was. Perhaps her sister was hurt and needed her.

Taking a deep breath, she flung open the door, finding Sebastian on the other side, his handsome face drawn and troubled.

She stumbled back, her heart dropping to her toes. "I'm s-sorry. I know I'm n-not decent. I just c-couldn't wait."

"You look..." He cut himself off and shook his head, tearing his gaze away from her scantily clad body and fixing it on a point over her shoulder. "My lady... Jocelyn... there's no easy way to say this..."

Something deep inside her seemed to shake apart, and it took her a moment to realize the wail of pain she heard was coming from her own lips. Her legs collapsed, but before she could hit the floor, he scooped her up in his arms, kicking the door shut behind him and carrying her across the room to the sofa, where he sank down, still holding her close.

"I'm sorry," he whispered into her hair. "I'm so sorry."

His words just made her cry harder because they finalized what she couldn't even put into words. The moment she'd seen his face, she'd known.

Evelyn was gone. She was never coming back.

SEBASTIAN CRADLED THE beautiful, damp, sobbing woman in his arms close, holding her as she cried for the sister she'd lost. He'd never felt so completely inadequate. He hadn't broken the news to her the way he should have, hadn't even been able to get the words out before she'd completely fallen apart.

He thought she'd somehow known all along, from the moment she'd shown up at his office yesterday morning. He believed in women's intuition, and the two sisters had obviously been incredibly close. From what she'd told him yesterday, Evelyn had been the only family Jocelyn had left except for her young son.

"I'm sorry, Jocelyn. I'm so sorry," he said again, loving the feel of her name on his lips, her silky damp hair against his face, her soft curves against his hard edges. She smelled delicious, like lavender and vanilla. He was a bastard for noticing such things when she was in so much pain, but how could he not? When she'd opened the door and he'd seen her standing there in nothing but a robe that clung wetly to every inch of her, it had been all he could do to get out any words at all.

It could have been five minutes or five hours that he held her as she cried, but at long last, her sobs subsided to hiccupping breathy gasps. "I'm getting your shirt all n-nasty," she finally managed.

"Don't worry about that," he whispered, his heart aching for her. "I'm just so sorry I had to be the one to come here and tell you this terrible thing."

"I'm glad it was you," she told him, curling her hand in the fabric of his shirt, suddenly sagging bonelessly against him, as if all the fight and emotion had gone completely out of her. "If it had to be anyone, I'm glad it was you."

He hugged her tightly, hoping against hope that she wouldn't ask any more questions, that he wouldn't have to tell her exactly what had happened to the lovely young woman who had been Jocelyn's sister until that monster had worked his murderous wiles on her.

"Tell me what happened," she whispered, making no move to leave the comfort of his lap.

He sighed, knowing that he had to tell her but searching for the right words. How could he tell a gently bred, aristocratic woman like Jocelyn what had been done to her sister? Could she ever get over such a thing? Although he'd seen such things more times than he cared to think about, it never got easier, and the women The Viper had brutalized haunted his dreams.

"She was in the gardener's shed in Postman's Park," he said quietly, brushing a few damp strands of lovely auburn hair from those tear-filled green eyes. "I should have broken the damned door down while we were there, but instead, it took an entire day for the gardener to be found. Then the key didn't work, and they had to cut the lock off anyway." He took a deep breath. "Someone murdered her, Jocelyn."

"Why?" Her eyes welled with fresh tears as she tried to

come to terms with what he was telling her. "Why would anyone do that to my sweet sister?"

He shook his head, unable to tell her the worst of it, not right now. He didn't want to tell her that it had been The Viper, nor that he had left a note with the word *whore* scrawled across it at her feet as he had with the girls from Mercy House.

Lady Evelyn Lindsay had obviously led a secret life that Jocelyn knew nothing about.

"I should go," he said, filled with new purpose. There were a million things he could be doing now that there was more evidence to process. He hoped to God that the bastard had made a mistake this time, left some evidence behind that would help them to figure out who he was.

"I know," she murmured, and he swore there was regret in her eyes. Did she want him to stay with her as much as he wished he could? "Thank you so much for coming, for being the one to tell me."

"I'm so sorry for your loss, Jocelyn." He wished like hell it had been anything but this that had brought him to her bedroom tonight. Still, he was glad he had been here to offer her comfort.

She turned her head in an attempt to keep him from seeing the fresh tears that welled up at his words, and his heart clenched once more for having been the one to cause them. Taking a deep, shuddering breath, she slid off his lap and stood in front of him, the light from the fire in the hearth dancing across her scantily clad figure.

"Please forgive my scandalous behavior... Sebastian," she told him, still unable to meet his gaze. "I'm afraid I was quite overcome."

"Don't apologize," he told her, getting reluctantly to his feet and staring down at her bowed head, her auburn hair still damp and falling wildly across her shoulders. He'd never seen anything quite so lovely or erotic. He wanted to press his mouth to that sweet spot at the base of her neck and simply breathe her in. "Is there anything else I can do for you before I go?"

"I need to make arrangements for her funeral, her burial."

"I'll let you know when the—when she can be released to the family."

"What do you mean?"

"The police are still gathering evidence from her. They'll need a few days." He said it as gently as he could.

"I... I don't know how this happened," she sobbed, shaking her head. "How c-could this happen to Evelyn, who was the sweetest of souls?"

"I don't know, but I promise I'll find out. I promise I'll find the bastard who did this." The words were a vow that he made not just to her but to himself.

She looked up at him then, those lovely eyes still full of tears, her rosy lips trembling. He'd never wanted to kiss a woman so badly, nor known more deeply that he couldn't. The sweet fire they'd kindled had to be halted. It was the last thing she needed right now.

"I believe you," she breathed. "I know you will."

No one in his entire life had ever put their faith in him the way this woman had, and he felt the weight of it to his toes. He would not let her down. He couldn't.

# Chapter Nine

After the inspector left, Jocelyn sat on the sofa in front of the fire, staring sightlessly into the flames as she struggled to come to grips with her new reality. All she had left was Oliver. Everyone else she'd ever loved, her entire family, was gone now. The thought of not having her sister to talk to, to laugh and cry with, was staggering.

She felt very alone in the world.

Thank goodness Sebastian had been the one to break the news to her. She'd never thought of herself as someone who would nearly pass out with grief, but she had been crippled with sadness and wouldn't have wanted anyone else to see her that way.

Why had it felt so natural to let herself sob in his arms? She'd never been that intimate with anyone, certainly not her husband. He had never once touched her unless it was to fumble under her nightgown and rut between her legs for a few minutes.

She grimaced at the thought, shaking it away.

There were things she'd need to do tomorrow. She'd have to make arrangements for a funeral, tell Abbie...

Perhaps she should go upstairs right now and wake Abbie; she certainly had a right to know. But the thought of actually saying the words crippled her. She needed a little more time to come to terms with it herself before she could even think of telling someone else.

She suddenly wished she hadn't gone looking for Evelyn yesterday. If she hadn't, her sister certainly wouldn't have been found yet, and she'd have had another night of blissful ignorance.

Tears welled in her eyes once again, and she doubled over, curling into a ball on the sofa and pulling the blanket over her. She didn't know how long she cried, but a gentle hand on her shoulder made her gasp and scramble to a sitting position again, blinking up at Abbie, who stood beside her in her nightclothes, wringing her hands with tears streaking down her face as well.

"I'm so sorry, ma'am. I know I shouldn't have come into your room, but I knocked, and you didn't answer, and I heard you crying..."

Jocelyn wiped her nose inelegantly with the back of her hand, wishing for a handkerchief. "It's all right, Abbie," she managed. "Thank you for checking on me."

Abbie bit her lip. "Winston said the inspector had come, and I knew he was looking for Evelyn, so I thought I'd come ask if she... she... Is she all right?" The look on Abbie's face said she already knew the answer to that, but Jocelyn forced herself to say it anyway.

"No, she's n-not all right, Abbie. She's been... m-murdered." The last word came out as more of a wail, and Jocelyn still couldn't believe she was saying such a thing about her dear, sweet sister.

Abbie gasped, then went white as a ghost as she sank down

on the sofa beside Jocelyn. "Murdered? How can she possibly have been murdered? Not Evelyn."

Jocelyn shook her head, wishing she'd asked Sebastian more questions. But perhaps she really didn't want to know the answers. Not yet, anyway.

She didn't know Abbie well, not like Evelyn had, but she knew the two women had a special connection and that Abbie was probably grieving nearly as much as she was. So she pulled the other girl tightly against her, and they held each other and cried for Evelyn until they both fell into an exhausted sleep.

BY THE TIME SEBASTIAN returned to Scotland Yard, Evelyn's body had already been brought in, and Dr. Chancy Lockwood was performing his autopsy. Blackstone was in his office, waiting for the doctor's report, and Sebastian wasn't surprised to find his old friend O'Brien had been summoned as well. Although O'Brien had retired after the horrible injury he'd suffered going after The Viper a few months ago, he still consulted with them from time to time.

"Ness," O'Brien greeted him tersely. "I wish we were meeting under different circumstances."

"So do I," Sebastian replied, sinking into the only unoccupied chair. "It's a terrible thing."

"How did Lady Aston take the news?" Blackstone asked, his dark eyes weary.

"About as well as you might expect," Sebastian said, trying to banish the thought of holding her while she cried. "She's devastated."

"Lady Evelyn was a fine lady." O'Brien shook his head. "All

my theories about who The Viper is have been crushed by this. It makes no sense that he'd go after a lady."

"I don't understand it either," Sebastian said. "Why would he accuse Lady Evelyn of being a whore like the others? By all accounts, she was a spinster who'd never been with a man."

O'Brien frowned. "Perhaps she rejected him? There seems to be some indication that the others The Viper killed had rejected him in some way."

Blackstone cleared his throat and shot to his feet, seeming a bit agitated. "Who would she have rejected? As a spinster, I'm sure she'd have welcomed a proposal from just about anyone."

Sebastian frowned. "It is possible hearsay and maybe even idle gossip with no basis in fact, but the victim confided in one of her friends that she had an unwelcome and persistent suitor and was determined to call him off that very night."

"This is a lady we're talking about," O'Brien protested. "A lady I personally knew. She would never have gone to meet someone by herself."

"Does the suitor have a name yet?" Blackstone asked Sebastian hurriedly.

"Not yet, sir. But I am pursuing that lead. Jocelyn had no idea of such a gentleman's existence, but someone must know something. Ladies talk about such things together, or at least I think they do. Whatever the victim did that night, I'm certain it was nothing improper on her part." Sebastian inwardly swore at himself for his slip of calling the countess by her given name, but neither of his companions seemed to notice. "I will go and speak to her again tomorrow."

He was worried about her and wanted to be certain she was all right.

Blackstone suddenly shook his head. "No. I think you're both wrong. There must be another answer. What if Lady Evelyn had a whole life that no one knew about? What if she truly was a whore and our killer was one of her lovers?"

Sebastian and O'Brien exchanged startled glances. Blackstone's instincts were usually spot on, but he didn't seem to be thinking clearly. Especially since Lady Evelyn had been a close personal friend of his.

"I want you to investigate that angle, Ness," Blackstone continued. "I think you've bothered Lady Aston enough. I'm sure she's already told you everything she knows."

Now Blackstone was forbidding him to talk to Jocelyn? That really made no sense.

O'Brien was undoubtedly still cursing the fact that his injury had taken him off the case, and Blackstone... Well, who knew what had set him off? But Sebastian knew that he was merely looking for an excuse to talk to Jocelyn again. She probably had told him everything she knew.

"Well, I do know one piece of information about our killer," Sebastian told the others, deciding not to argue the point at the moment. "One of his initials seems to be M."

Blackstone gave an explosive laugh. "What do you mean? How do you know that?"

"In her diary, Lady Evelyn said she was meeting with someone named 'M' at Postman's Park. Someone who had once asked for her hand in marriage and been turned down. Someone who had sent her notes saying that he wanted her to change her mind. I highly doubt that 'M' and the killer are two different men."

Blackstone shook his head. "We don't know if that refers

to a first initial, a last initial, or a title. There are probably more than a dozen members of The Viper Club who have an M in their name. Hell, by that criteria, it could be me."

Sebastian and O'Brien exchanged a startled look, to which Blackstone hurriedly said, "My point is, it could be anyone for all the progress that has been made. The initial M? That's all you've got?"

Sebastian said, "We're exploring every far-flung theory, only because this case is so confounding."

"We *don't* think you're The Viper," O'Brien said cautiously to Blackstone. "But even if it narrows it down a little bit, it's worth pursuing past or potential suitors. Especially if one of those men was ever rejected by Lady Evelyn."

"I agree with you, sir. There are a bevy of suspects if we consider any man who ever knew her, even casually, the initial M notwithstanding, for it could even be a nickname," Sebastian added. "For all we know, M could stand for milliner."

Sebastian watched Blackstone warily, feeling more confused by the moment. Surely, there was no reason to suspect him. So, why was he acting so strangely?

Blackstone ran his hand through his hair in frustration. "Forgive me, lads. I'm just upset about Lady Evelyn. She was a long-time friend, and I can't believe this happened in Mayfair. We're going to be under a lot more pressure than we were before, and it was killing me before."

Sebastian nodded. "The pressure is getting to me, too. But we've had so little to work with until now, I'm happy to have an initial. It will narrow down the pool a little, and maybe that's all we need."

"Let me interview Lady Aston," Blackstone insisted again.

"She's undoubtedly taking this very hard, and I think I can be a little gentler with her than either of you."

*I was pretty damn gentle with her earlier tonight.* The memory of holding her soft, sweet body so tenderly in his arms crashed back over him, and he shifted uncomfortably. The last thing he wanted was Blackstone reminding him how little he belonged in her world.

And the thought of Blackstone holding her the way he had made him want to hit something.

A knock on the door interrupted that train of thought as a constable came in to tell them that the doctor had finished his work on Lady Evelyn.

The three of them followed the constable down into the bowels of the building, where the doctor did his gruesome work. O'Brien stopped outside the door to light a cigarette, a trick some men in their line of work used to mask the smell of death, but Sebastian had never resorted to such measures. During his time in the army, he'd gotten used to it.

It was amazing what one could get used to.

Once inside the cold, grim room, he found a body lying on a steel table, a neat cross of stitches across her chest and abdomen. He tried not to look at her face. The girl he'd met at the wedding was long gone. This desecrated shell was something else altogether.

The doctor leaned against the counter, a grim look on his face. "I'm afraid this one is just like the others. The laceration to the trachea was the cause of death. The rest of her injuries were done post-mortem. Nothing else that can help you."

"Nothing else that can help us?" Blackstone shouted. "What the hell are we paying you for?"

The doctor straightened, a haughty look settling across his grim features. "I can only find what's there to find. Your killer isn't leaving anything behind."

Frustration built within Sebastian until he felt that he'd explode. How was it possible that The Viper had now committed three murders, and they weren't any closer to finding out his identity than they'd been after the first one? No wonder Blackstone was acting so strangely.

O'Brien sighed and turned for the door. "Let's go talk this over at the pub, Ness."

Sebastian nodded grimly, and the two men silently left the building, heading down the street to their favorite pub. Neither of them said a word until they'd settled in a booth near the back with frothy pints setting in front of them.

"What the hell is wrong with Blackstone?" O'Brien asked at last. "He doesn't seem himself."

"I thought the same," Sebastian agreed, glad he wasn't the only one who'd thought the entire exchange had been strange. "Perhaps he's just upset about Lady Evelyn. I doubt he's ever had to deal with the murder of someone in his own circle."

O'Brien nodded and drank deeply, staring at a spot over Sebastian's head as he obviously tried to work it all out in his head. "This is a hell of a thing."

"I can't stop thinking that we should know who it is, that there's a clue we're missing. I think we should talk about Prometheus again." He took a deep breath, about to explain once again why his theory made sense. The bastard who'd thrown O'Brien off the back of that carriage and had caused his injury had been wearing a cloak and the Prometheus mask, for God's sake.

But O'Brien held up a hand, stopping him. "You have to let go of that idea," he said firmly. "I can't tell you how, but I know with one hundred percent certainty that Prometheus is not The Viper."

"How could you possibly...?" Sebastian trailed off. "You know who Prometheus is, don't you?"

O'Brien nodded grimly. "For quite some time now, actually."

The look of pained loyalty on his friend's face made the last of the pieces fall into place. "It's one of your brothers-in-law, isn't it?"

"Someone used the Prometheus mask to throw us off their trail," O'Brien said, and the fact that he didn't deny Sebastian's accusation was not lost on him. "Prometheus has been a friend to us, helping clean up places that sold children for nefarious purposes. While I haven't always appreciated his methods, I can't argue with his results."

Nodding, Sebastian sank back against his seat. "I suppose you're right. But damn it. That leaves us with nothing."

"A snuffbox. A woman who is nothing like the others. The location of Postman's Park, his familiarity with the gardener's cottage." O'Brien grimaced. "I've been over this in my head a million times, and adding Evelyn Lindsay to the bastard's victims makes no sense."

"Well, we better figure it out. We have to catch this bastard," Sebastian said grimly. "I simply cannot abide this monster killing again."

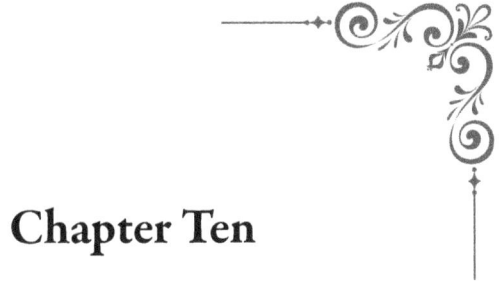

# Chapter Ten

Jocelyn spent the next day drifting throughout her house, dry-eyed and numb, wondering why she couldn't cry. Was there a limit to the tears one could expend? She felt worn out by her grief, completely drained.

She hadn't told Oliver yet, and so far, he hadn't asked where his aunt was, but she knew it was only a matter of time. What would she say then?

How did one explain such a thing to a three-year-old?

Just after four, her butler found her in the parlor to let her know that Drake Blackstone had arrived to speak to her. Despite everything, a surge of disappointment went through her. Though she'd known Drake most of her life, she'd much rather he'd sent Sebastian Ness.

Drake was shown into the parlor, and his eyes were filled with sympathy as he took the chair across from her. "I'm so sorry for your loss."

"Thank you." The tears she hadn't been able to find all morning immediately welled up, and she blinked rapidly, embarrassed to be giving in to them now. Why was it that she didn't want her old friend to see her in a moment of weakness, but she'd so willingly gone into Sebastian Ness's arms and cried her eyes out last night?

Drake cleared his throat. "I just came by to let you know that we're doing everything we can to ensure that this monster is brought to justice. I won't let another woman suffer at The Viper's hands."

"The Viper?" Jocelyn shook her head, horror rushing through her, a cold sweat breaking out all over her body. "Evelyn was killed by The Viper?"

With a wince, Drake leaned forward and took her hand. "I thought you knew. I thought Ness had told you. I'm so sorry."

"But I don't understand," Jocelyn said, her voice rising with every word. Why *hadn't* Sebastian told her? Had it been some sort of misguided attempt to protect her? "I thought The Viper only killed prostitutes."

It was bad enough to know that Evelyn had been murdered. But to know she'd been a victim of *The Viper?* She'd seen the salacious news stories, the graphic details of how the killer brutalized his victims. She'd even heard firsthand from Allison, who'd discovered The Viper's first victim.

Nausea welled within her, and she surged to her feet. "I can't... I don't...." Unable to get anything else out, she turned and ran from the room, barely able to reach the water closet down the hall before she cast up the little she'd managed to eat today.

Sobbing, she sank to the floor, visions of what must have happened to sweet, gentle Evelyn filling her brain until she wanted to crush her own skull just to get rid of them. How had this happened? Why? Evelyn had nothing in common with those other girls The Viper had murdered.

She didn't know how much time had gone by before a soft knock sounded at the door. "Jocelyn? Are you...? Can I do anything to help?"

More tears squeezed out at the sound of Drake's voice. Once again, she wished it had been Sebastian who'd come to speak to her today. She felt as though she were about to shake apart, and Sebastian Ness was the only glue that might put her back together. It made no sense, but neither did anything else that had happened in the last three days.

"There's nothing you can do," she told him brokenly. "Please, I just want to be alone."

He said nothing for a long moment, then cleared his throat. "Let me know if you need anything. And I do need to ask you some questions. About... what happened."

Another sob escaped her, and then she heard his footsteps retreating.

He had questions? Well, so did she. She had a million questions. But she had a really bad feeling that she was never going to know the answers to any of them.

WHEN JOCELYN FINALLY emerged from the water closet half an hour later, she was dry-eyed once again. Would this continue to happen? Hours of numbness followed by bouts of crippling grief?

Feeling as though she was a ghost haunting her own house, she drifted up the stairs to the nursery on the third floor. She usually kept Oliver with her a good part of the day, but she still didn't know what to say to him, and she didn't want him to see her crying.

However, she was sure her little boy was missing her, and she also knew it wasn't fair to make Abbie watch him all day when she was grieving for Evelyn, too.

She stood in the doorway for a minute, listening as Abbie read Oliver's favorite book to him and thought how lucky both she and Evelyn had been to have had Abbie in their lives. Jocelyn knew Abbie loved Oliver almost as much as she did.

When the story was done, she went inside, smiling when Oliver rushed over to her on his chubby little legs. Scooping him up in her arms, she met Abbie's watery gaze. "Why don't you take the rest of the day off, Abbie?"

Abbie's eyes widened in surprise, but then she nodded vigorously. "Thank you, my lady."

Once Abbie had gone, Jocelyn carried Oliver, who was already blinking tiredly, over to his small bed and laid down beside him. "Let's take a little nap, shall we?" she coaxed, hugging him tightly against her.

Grabbing a chunk of her hair, he closed his eyes and was soon sleeping soundly.

The terrible truth was that she'd been glad when Albert had died. There had been no love between them whatsoever. He'd been cruel, forbidding her to leave the house unless he accompanied her but largely ignoring her except to criticize or bed her.

But then Allison had fallen in love with Quinn O'Brien, waxing poetically about how incredible it was to be in his arms. Jocelyn had never thought she'd feel anything remotely similar to what her friend had described, but then she'd found herself wanting to kiss the inspector's cheek. And once she had, she'd wanted to kiss his mouth. And then she'd started to want so much more. She'd wanted to explore all these overwhelming feelings and desire with the man who'd made her feel them.

She shifted restlessly, overwhelmed with guilt. She shouldn't be thinking about these sorts of things when she'd just found out that her sister was dead. She shouldn't have been thinking of them at all, because the last thing in the world she wanted was another man in her life.

But he'd held her so tenderly last night...

With a groan, she pulled a nearby pillow over her head, trying to banish all thoughts of the handsome inspector. Her sister was dead, and if she must think about a man, she'd be better served trying to figure out who "M" was, because he was one who'd lured Evelyn to the park and killed her.

Evelyn and Jocelyn had spoken every day. Jocelyn had always told her sister everything, so how was it possible that Evelyn had been going through something like this and never told her about it? It hurt to know that her sister hadn't felt she could trust her with such a thing.

If only Evelyn had come to her, if only she'd asked her to go with her that night, perhaps she could have stopped this terrible thing from happening.

# Chapter Eleven

During the next two days, Sebastian only got a few hours of sleep. He'd been called to meetings with more people than he could count, gone over the evidence with Blackstone and O'Brien until he thought he'd go mad, and interviewed dozens of people. The reporters had learned who The Viper's latest victim was, and the reverberations from that had traveled through the city like a lightning bolt. Reporters clustered around police headquarters like a flock of crows, hungry for any tidbit of new information.

People were afraid. They were demanding the killer be caught.

He didn't blame them, but it disgusted him that no one had been this incensed when it was just a couple of dead prostitutes. Why was one human life considered so much more valuable than another?

Through it all, his mind drifted repeatedly to Jocelyn.

He wanted to know if she was all right. He also wanted to know if she'd added anyone else to the list he'd asked for, of all the men in Evelyn's life who had an initial of M.

Blackstone had apparently gone to see her, but he claimed she'd been overcome by emotion, and he hadn't been able to question her at all. Perhaps that was true, but she might be the key to the information that would help him find her sister's killer. He didn't know her that well, but he somehow doubted that now, two days later, she was still incapable of answering a few questions or completing the list. In fact, he'd lay odds that she wanted more than anything to help them.

So, even though he was exhausted and wanted nothing more than to return to his rented rooms in Bethnal Green and finally get some sleep, he found himself on her doorstep two days after the last time he'd been there. To his dismay, he had to push past several reporters to get to her door while they shouted questions he had no intention of answering.

Damned vultures. Jocelyn was dealing with enough. She didn't need to look out her windows and see these bastards lying in wait.

The butler no longer looked surprised to see him. He ushered him inside and slammed the door in the reporters' faces, then escorted him into the parlor while he went to get his mistress.

With a sigh, Sebastian sank down on the comfortable blue sofa in front of the fire, stretching his long legs out toward the warmth and letting his head fall back against the soft fabric as he waited for her.

He didn't even realize he'd fallen asleep until he woke up. The room was dark, lit only by the bright flames of the fire, and he was warmer than he'd been in days, covered from chin to toes by a heavy quilted blanket. He blinked and scrambled to sit up fully, only to realize that Jocelyn sat beside him, her head against his shoulder.

Her own owlish look as they stared at each other made him realize that she must have fallen asleep as well. Embarrassment filled him. He'd come here to check in on her and then ask her some questions, not fall asleep on her sofa. But as the blanket fell away from his arms, he realized that she must have been the one to cover him up, and that was the most thoughtful thing anyone had done for him in ages. In fact, had anyone ever taken care of him in such a manner? Marina certainly hadn't, and he wasn't even certain his own mother, who'd always seemed to think of him as a terrible nuisance, had.

"You looked so tired," she said softly, and even in the dim light, he could tell she was blushing. "I didn't think you'd been getting much sleep, and I didn't want to wake you. I didn't mean to lean against you, but I haven't been sleeping much either."

"It's all right." He cleared his throat, wishing he wouldn't have startled her awake. "I just came by to see how you were doing."

She gave a hollow laugh. "Some moments I'm fine, others I feel numb, and sometimes I'm a complete watering pot."

"I imagine it will be like that for some time," he said, wanting nothing more than to pull her back into his arms and hold her until her beautiful smile returned.

She nodded, blinking back a sudden rush of tears. "Have you found the man who did this yet?"

He shook his head, feeling like an utter failure. "I'm afraid he didn't leave any clues to his identity. I was hoping that you'd been thinking about who 'M' could be."

"I have." She scrambled to her feet and crossed the room, turning on a gas lamp as she did so and flooding the room with its glaring white light.

He put his hand over his eyes, blinded for a moment, and

when he lowered it, she stood before him with a sheet of paper in her hands. "Here's everyone I could think of who has the initial M." She sat back down beside him and pointed to the neatly organized page, which held far more names than her first scribbled list had. "This column is those with the first name M, these are the ones whose last names start with M, and the last row of those whose title starts with M."

Sebastian groaned inwardly. There were nearly as many names on this list as there were members of The Viper Club. And once again, nearly all of them were aristocrats who would be very hard to question, including his boss, his boss's brother, and O'Brien's brother-in-law, Morgan Strathmore. But there had to be some names that were on both lists, and that would be the best place to start.

"Thank you." He tried to summon a smile. "This is very helpful."

"I can't believe anyone on that list could do such a thing, could be The Viper! But Evelyn obviously knew him well enough to agree to meet him alone at the park, so I can only assume that it's someone I knew as well." Her eyes were liquid green pools of sadness. "I just still can't believe she's gone."

Her voice broke on the last word, and he lost his battle to keep from taking her in his arms. Lifting the side of the blanket closest to her, he scooted toward her, pulled her against his side, and wrapped the blanket around them both. "It will be all right," he whispered, placing a tender kiss against her lovely auburn hair. "Everything will be all right."

"No, it won't," she sobbed, stiffening for just a moment before turning her face against his chest and wrapping one arm around his waist. "I'm all alone in the world now except for

Oliver. Nothing will ever be all right again."

There was nothing he could say to that because he was all alone in the world too, and it was the worst feeling, even though he should be used to it. Instead, he just held her while she cried once again, wishing he could do something more.

After a few minutes, her sobs abated, and he could tell she was valiantly trying to regain control of herself. He wanted to tell her not to bother, but she was a prideful little thing, and he knew she probably hated herself for once again breaking down in front of him.

"I want to do whatever I can to help you find this bastard," she finally said, her use of profanity shocking him a bit. If he knew one thing about Jocelyn Layton, it was that she strove to be a perfect lady at all times. But perhaps when said bastard had killed your sister, it was acceptable to be a little crass. "Do you need to ask me any more questions?"

He'd asked her so many questions the day they'd been searching for Evelyn, but when he'd been asking them, he'd never really thought anything bad had happened to the poor woman. Now everything looked different, and it probably wouldn't hurt to ask her some of them again.

"I do," he said softly, squeezing her a little tighter. "But let's just sit here for a moment first so I can get my wits about me."

She gave a choking little chuckle but then nodded, and the last of her resistance seemed to fade as she went absolutely boneless against him.

"No one has ever held me this way," she whispered after a long while. "No one has ever given me any physical comfort whatsoever. Now you've done it several times in a matter of days, just when I needed it the very most. Thank you."

"You're welcome," he said simply, tamping back the rest of the words that suddenly wanted to spill out. He wanted to tell her that he'd gained something from it as well, that she'd soothed a bit of the monster that raged within him at his inability to keep this from happening, that he felt guilty for not having caught the bastard before he struck again. But none of it made any sense. They were practically strangers, yet he'd never felt this close to anyone. Not even his wife.

She nestled a little bit closer, and for the first time tonight, a surge of a different kind of warmth moved through him. She just felt so sweet and soft against him, all lovely curves, fragrant skin, and fiery hair. Calling once again on every shred of willpower he possessed, he tried to will his body back into submission. If she noticed how much she affected him, all her trust would vanish like smoke in the wind, and for the first time in his life, he found he wanted this woman's trust and friendship more than her body.

"I didn't get much physical affection when I was young either," he told her slowly, surprised he was sharing this with her. He usually kept the details of his personal life secret, even from those he was closest to. "I married when I was very young. Her name was Marina. We'd only been wed a few days before I went off to the Army, but she was very affectionate... Not just in the bedroom, but like this... I'd never known what I was missing, how it felt to be close to someone. I craved it so much when I was away."

It had been so long since he'd spoken of Marina. So long since he'd let himself feel any of this.

She tensed, all of her lovely pliancy suddenly disappearing. "You're married?"

"No," he hastened to assure her. "I'm a widower. She died a long time ago."

She heaved a deep sigh but relaxed again. "Oh, Sebastian. I'm so sorry."

He didn't tell her that Marina had run off with another man while he was gone. That she'd died giving birth to that man's baby. It was all so tawdry, something a woman like her could never understand.

Another period of silence passed between them, but then she cleared her throat and pulled away from him with what seemed like reluctance. "I'm ready now. Ask me whatever you need to."

He stared into her resolute, tear-streaked face and thought he'd never seen anything so brave. He wanted to kiss her. He wanted to make all of this go away for a while longer, but since she was being so brave, he had to honor that.

"I don't know how to say this delicately." He frowned, trying to find the words to ask her what he needed to know. "The Viper's other victims were all women who had been his former lovers—"

"What are you saying?" Jocelyn pushed to her feet, suddenly vibrating with anger. "Are you asking me if Evelyn..." She broke off, shaking her head in disgust. "No. Absolutely not. I told you before. Evelyn was not involved with any man."

He winced, knowing he'd gone about this all wrong. "I know that you want to believe that. But if she was, it's possible you didn't know about it. That's something she might not have shared with you. She might have wanted to keep it a secret."

"My sister and I didn't keep secrets from each other!" She drew herself up to her full five-foot height and looked down her nose at him, suddenly every bit the countess. "I want to help you find whoever did this, but I won't let you malign my sister's character is such a way."

"I'm not trying to malign her character. But if she had a lover, we need to know who it was." He got to his feet as well, feeling awkward. "I won't think less of her. I won't think anything at all. I just want a name so I can make this bastard pay for what he's done."

"Well, you'll have to find another way, because there is no man. I am absolutely positive of that."

He took a deep breath. "The killer left a piece of paper with one word on it at Evelyn's feet. Do you know what that word was?"

She shook her head, her eyes daring him to say it.

He swallowed. "It was *whore*, Jocelyn. Does that sound like something that he would have left if there wasn't some sort of personal relationship between them?"

"Get out," she said, her emerald eyes snapping fire.

"I'm sorry, I know it hurts to hear such things, and I could be wrong. But I wouldn't be doing my job if I didn't at least ask, just to rule it—"

"I want you to leave," she repeated, trembling with fury. "Is this the only reason you came here tonight? To malign my sister's reputation and make these insinuations?"

Her hurt and anger slayed him. The last thing he'd wanted was to cast aspersions on the dead girl, but he needed to rule it out. He wanted to defend himself and his intentions, calm her down, but he could tell by the look on her face that she wasn't going to listen to him. Not today. He'd committed an unpardonable mistake.

"I will go," he said stiffly. "But please, don't hesitate to reach out to me if you think of anything that might help me catch the bastard who did this."

"You can see yourself out." Without another word, she turned and left the room, leaving him feeling dazed, lost, and guilty.

# Chapter Twelve

J ocelyn slammed her bedroom door shut and leaned against it, breathing heavily with tears streaking down her cheeks. She couldn't believe she'd let herself get so comfortable with that man, actually leaned against him and cried in his arms. Let him touch her and kiss her. When all along, he'd only wanted to ask her those disgusting questions about Evelyn.

*Whore.*

The word reverberated in her mind, making her feel sick. Had the killer really left that note at Evelyn's feet? Had he used her in an unspeakable way before killing her?

The mere thought made the bile at the back of her throat rise up, and she barely made it to the bathroom before casting up her accounts once again. Sobbing, she leaned over the water closet, her heart breaking for what her poor sister had gone through.

Wonderful, sweet Evelyn. How could someone have done this to her, let alone someone she'd known and trusted?

Her mind raced over the list she'd made. She couldn't imagine a single person on that list who could have done such a thing. Was it possible the inspector had things all wrong and it had been someone else, a stranger, who'd lured Evelyn to the park and killed her?

But why would a stranger choose Evelyn, of all people? Did it have something to do with her work with the women's suffrage movement? With the secret that she'd kept for the last few years?

Either of those things might have stirred the ire of a psychotic misogynist.

She moved slowly to the sink, rinsing her mouth out and then staring at herself in the mirror for several long minutes, hardly recognizing the wan, crazed-looking woman she'd become.

*You're angry because you like him. Because you were starting to trust him.*

Shaking her head, she left the bathroom and flopped down on her bed, staring sightlessly at the ceiling. As the minutes ticked by, her anger drained away, replaced by grief and desolation once again.

*Oh, Evelyn. I don't know how I'm going to make it without you.*

A soft knock on her door sent her scrambling to sit up. "Come in," she called hoarsely.

Abbie opened the door a crack and peeked in at her. "I saw that the inspector just left. I was just wondering if he had any news?"

The poor girl looked just as bad as Jocelyn did. Her face was red and patchy, her eyes swollen and bloodshot.

Jocelyn gestured for her to come inside, and Abbie did so, shutting the door behind her.

She knew that what had happened would hurt Abbie as much as it had herself, but she needed to know. Perhaps she might know something that even Jocelyn didn't.

"He wanted to ask me questions. They think..." Jocelyn cleared her throat, still unable to believe what he'd asked. "He thinks that Evelyn had a lover and that he was the one who lured her to the park and killed her. He said that the killer left the word *whore* on a piece of paper at her feet."

Abbie gasped, her dark eyes widening. "But she didn't... She wasn't... We know that isn't possible."

"Yes," Jocelyn agreed. "But we can't tell him *how* we know that. Besides, it has nothing to do with what happened, and it's none of his business."

"Thank you for trying to protect her. To protect us." Abbie smiled wanly through her tears and shook her head. "But you need to tell him, my lady. As long as he is stuck on this theory, he won't be able to see anything else."

"But I don't want to risk—"

"It doesn't matter," Abbie cut her off. "None of it matters anymore. But I understand if you don't want to bring more shame upon your family."

Jocelyn shook her head fiercely. "I'm not ashamed of anything Evelyn did. She was the best person I knew, and I supported every decision she made."

Flushing even darker, Abbie gave her a grateful look. "Then tell him. He needs to know so he can find out who did this to her."

"If you're certain," Jocelyn said doubtfully. "I still don't think it's necessary."

"If you don't, I will," Abbie said, squaring her shoulders. "I want whoever did this to pay."

"I'll tell him," Jocelyn relented with a sigh. "I want The Viper caught and punished as well."

Abbie nodded and left, and Jocelyn went about her ablutions without ringing for her maid. She still felt jittery with emotion, and she didn't want to have to put on a brave face because she wasn't feeling at all brave.

By the time she crawled under the blankets, she had worked herself into quite a state once again. On the one hand, she knew Abbie was right, that she had to tell the inspector why she was so certain it hadn't been Evelyn's lover who'd killed her, but she still felt stung by what he'd implied.

*He's just doing his job.*

She knew it was true, but it had just been so hard to hear such things after the sweet moment of tenderness and sharing that had just passed between them. Now that she was safe in her bed, she had to admit that it had perhaps been the most emotionally charged moment of her life.

Sebastian Ness was nothing she'd ever thought she'd want in a man. He was far below her station, and his career, though necessary, was crass and dangerous. So why had he been on her mind so much since she'd met him?

She closed her eyes, thinking of his beautiful eyes and sensual smile. The way he'd kissed her and given her pleasure. The way he'd held her, making her feel safe for the first time in her life.

Was that it? Did she secretly yearn for someone to make her feel safe? Someone who cared for her enough to keep her from harm?

The only problem with that was the fact that every hurt she'd ever suffered had been caused by a man. She'd thought that both her father and husband would have her best interests at heart, that they'd take care of her and cherish her. But her father had never cared about anything except the connections that her marriage could bring him, and her husband had never cared about anything but getting an heir before he died.

She was foolish to have thought, even for a moment, that Sebastian Ness could be any different.

AFTER LEAVING JOCELYN, Sebastian took a hack back to his flat in Bethnal Green. As he let himself into the small suite of rooms on the second floor of the brick tenement, he looked around at the faded wallpaper and simple furniture and shook his head in wry amusement that he'd ever thought that a woman from Mayfair might want to be involved with him at any level.

Shivering, he lit a fire in the hearth, then put a pot of water on the stove to make some tea. For a while, the activity kept his mind off what had just happened, but the moment he sat down in his worn yet comfortable chair in front of the fire, Jocelyn's tear-streaked, furious face haunted his thoughts.

He'd never meant to hurt her, and he still couldn't believe he'd let his emotions rule him enough to say those things about her sister. His questions had been necessary, but he should have taken her at her word and not pushed it. She'd obviously told him what she thought to be the truth, and no amount of digging was going to get her to change her mind.

If Evelyn Lindsay had taken a lover or gotten herself involved in something far more controversial than participating in the women's suffrage movement, she hadn't told her sister about it.

Taking a sip of his tea, he fished the list Jocelyn had made of the people in Evelyn's life who had the initial M out of his pocket, then reached for the list of members of The Viper Club. He was very aware that Jocelyn's list might not be complete. Evelyn could have known someone with the initial M that Jocelyn had never met. Still, after a half an hour of poring over the lists, he had seven names that appeared on both.

Unfortunately, Blackwood, his older brother Viscount Danbury, and O'Brien's brother-in-law Morgan Strathmore were three of those names.

No wonder Blackwood had been so upset the other day.

Sebastian would like to rule the three men out just because he knew them, but even if he did, the other four men were just as powerful, just as untouchable. Two of them had titles, and the other two were the sons of titled men.

He'd have a hard time interviewing any of them.

And experience had taught him that even the people you knew best could do unspeakable things. Did anyone ever truly know even those closest to them?

Anger roiled within him, and he finally tossed the papers aside in frustration. Why would a man like one of these, one who'd been born with a silver spoon in his mouth and never wanted for anything, start murdering young women as a pastime?

*Sex. Money. Revenge.*

Those seemed to be the main reasons people committed murder, and he and O'Brien had tried to examine The Viper killings from all three angles. The Viper hadn't raped the girls before killing them, so that ruled out sex. There was no indication that either of the two girls from Mercy House had anything worth stealing, and while Evelyn Lindsay might have had some assets, he didn't think that the killer had taken anything from her either. He'd have to ask Jocelyn about that... if she ever talked to him again.

Which just left revenge.

O'Brien had said something interesting while they'd been in the morgue. He'd said that the women might all have rejected The Viper, and that made sense from the one lead he had, that Evelyn had been going to meet a man whose proposal she'd once rejected. It certainly fit the motive that had claimed The Viper's other victims.

His gaze fell once again to the list he'd just made.

Had Evelyn rejected one of these men? Or even all of them? By all accounts, she was a spinster, a bluestocking. To most people, that meant no man had ever wanted her. But was it possible that one of these men had actually asked for her hand and she turned him down? Her father had been an earl. She'd likely had a decent dowry, and though nowhere near as lovely as her sister, she hadn't been hard on the eyes either.

The more that he thought about it, the odder it seemed that absolutely no one had wanted to marry Evelyn. Why had she chosen to be a bluestocking, rather than choosing a husband from among even the most modest of prospects?

He cursed himself for having tried to ask Jocelyn any questions tonight. If he'd only bid her goodbye after comforting her and had come home and figured this out, he could have gone to see her in the morning with the right question to ask, instead of one that had rightly infuriated her.

*Was your sister a whore?*

Of course, she was angry. If his new theory was true, it

could explain the killer's anger. No man wanted to believe that a woman would rather die a spinster than accept his suit. And he knew all too well how men liked to believe the worst about women who didn't find them worthy. Much easier to brand a woman a whore than to accept that she simply didn't want you.

With a groan, he got to his feet and went to his bedroom, shedding his suit and then collapsing on his bed in his small clothes. Shivering, he pulled a heavy quilt on top of him and stared up at the ceiling as he admitted for the first time how empty his life had become.

For the first few years after he'd left the army, it had been strange to be in a place of his own, instead of surrounded by others all the time. At first, he'd enjoyed the solitude, glad not to have to listen to snores and farts all night long. But very soon, the charm of being alone wore off, and he found himself missing the camaraderie, the friendship, the feeling of working toward a common goal.

He'd enjoyed his police work at first as well, but as the years had dragged on, he'd stopped feeling that he was making a difference, instead seeing it all as a somewhat desperate attempt to put his fingers in the holes of a leaking dyke. Every time he plugged one, it seemed that ten more opened up. His life had become a constant dance of contorting himself to plug those holes—a lonely dance, made even more so once O'Brien had left.

But he'd never before felt like he'd failed as utterly as he did tonight, knowing that Evelyn Lindsay might still be here if he'd simply manage to figure out who The Viper was and stop him in the months he'd had to do so.

Frustration surged through him, and his mind turned once

again to Jocelyn crying in his arms, her sorrow for her sister pouring out of her in a painful wave. He'd felt every single one of her tears, and he'd have done nearly anything to bear her pain for her.

He hadn't had these sort of feelings for a woman since Marina had broken his heart all those years ago. He'd thought that Marina had taken every bit of tenderness and passion with her when she'd left him.

But perhaps some lingering kernel of it remained.

He knew it was absolutely ridiculous to be having those feelings for this particular woman. They were worlds apart, and there was nothing he could do to change that. Just because his friend had found a way to be with a woman of the *ton* didn't mean that he and Jocelyn could ever do the same.

But perhaps the time had come to look for another, more suitable woman to give his heart to. Maybe it was time to stop coming home to an empty flat. He'd always thought he wanted children, but he was thirty years old, and if he was going to ever become a father, it was probably time to get started.

The thought brought him a strange measure of peace.

Perhaps Jocelyn had come into his life just to show him that it was possible to care about a woman again.

# Chapter Thirteen

The next morning, Jocelyn had her driver take her to Allison's house in Belgravia. She badly needed to talk to someone, and now that Evelyn was gone, Allison was the closest person in the world to her.

She'd spent most of the night trying to make sense of what had happened between herself and Sebastian and come to some sort of peace with what had been done to Evelyn, and she was exhausted. None of it made sense to her, and if she didn't give voice to some of the crazy thoughts whirling around in her mind, she was afraid her head might literally explode.

As she mounted the steps to Allison's front door, she realized she should have sent word ahead, but it seemed that since her friend had gotten married, Jocelyn had found herself breaking one rule of etiquette after another. And to her surprise, she didn't really care anymore. Her life had been turned upside down. What good were calling cards and seating arrangements? All of that seemed so petty and insignificant now.

It seemed impossible to believe that just a month ago, she'd been incensed at the idea of sitting at a round table with no place cards. What a fool she'd been. She should have enjoyed that night with her sister. She should have asked more about her work for the suffrage movement, actually paid attention to her sister when she spoke about the things she was passionate about.

The butler showed her into the parlor, and a few minutes later, Allison rushed into the room, her blue eyes full of sympathy. "Jocelyn. I'm so glad you came! I heard about what happened to Evelyn. I wanted to come see you, but I wasn't certain if you were ready to talk to anyone." She sank down to the sofa beside Jocelyn and pulled her into a warm embrace.

Jocelyn immediately burst into tears, so glad to have her friend's love and concern. It felt wonderful to be hugged. Perhaps this was all she needed. Surely, Allison's embrace would give her the same peace that Sebastian's had.

But after a few moments, she pulled away, realizing that was not the case. It was nice to be in Allison's arms, but it felt nowhere near as warm and comforting as it had to be held by Sebastian Ness.

Wiping her eyes, Jocelyn gave her friend a watery smile. "I still can't believe she's gone. How could this have happened?"

Before Allison could answer, her handsome, golden-haired husband, Quinn O'Brien, entered the room, his green eyes haunted. "Lady Aston. I was so sorry to hear of your loss."

Jocelyn knew that he'd most likely done more than just hear of Evelyn's death. Though he'd left the police after he'd been injured in his pursuit of The Viper, he still worked with Inspector Ness regularly on The Viper case. He'd no doubt been present during Evelyn's autopsy, the thought of which made her fight not to be sick yet again.

Though she knew it was necessary, she hated the thought of men poking, prodding, and cutting Evelyn's defenseless naked body.

"Thank you, Mr. O'Brien," she managed, nodding at Allison's husband.

"Please," he murmured. "We're practically family now. Call me Quinn."

Her face heated, because once again, this was highly inappropriate, but she nodded. "Only if you call me Jocelyn."

"I'll let the two of you talk," he said, giving his wife a fond look. "I just wanted to step in and let you know that if you need anything, anything at all, to let me know. I know how close the two of you are, and I want you to feel that you can count on me as much as you do Allison."

"I appreciate that," Jocelyn said, grateful for the show of support. For a moment, it occurred to her that perhaps this was who she should tell Evelyn's secret to. But something stopped her. And she realized that it was because despite everything, she wanted to see Sebastian again. She wondered what that said about her, what dreadful lack in her character it showed. "But at this point, I don't think there's anything anyone can do."

He left them, but Allison's gaze followed him until he was out of sight down the hall.

"Married life is obviously treating you well," Jocelyn observed, fighting down a little twinge of jealousy. She'd feared Allison might regret her decision, once she'd had some time to think about it, once a little of the new had worn off. But by all indications, nothing could be further from the truth.

Allison nodded, though she looked slightly guilty, which was the last thing Jocelyn wanted. Even though she'd been very unlucky in love, she was thrilled for her friend. For the first time, she wondered if her thoughts on love had been completely wrong, based only on her own experience. Would she have felt entirely different if her father had married her to a man like Sebastian?

She was almost certain that would have changed things profoundly.

"Every day that we spend together is better than the last," Allison admitted, her cheeks bright red. "I honestly never thought I would find someone who could make me feel so safe and cared for."

"That's good. I'm so happy for you," Jocelyn said softly, knowing that the red in her friend's cheeks was undoubtedly due to their physical relationship. She wanted to know every detail, but now was not the time. But it also struck her that Allison had used the word safe, which summed up how she'd started to feel about Sebastian.

Until he'd called her sister a whore. How could she ever trust him again after that?

Allison cleared her throat, obviously trying to tamp down her enthusiasm over her marriage. "But you are not here to talk about that," she said brusquely.

Jocelyn sighed. "I'm afraid not."

"What can I do?" Allison asked softly. "What do you need, Jocelyn?"

That was a good question. One that Jocelyn only had one answer for. "I need to know who did this to my sister. I need someone to believe me when I say that Evelyn was not some... *whore.*"

The ugly word stung her tongue, and she still couldn't believe that Sebastian had even hinted at such a thing to her.

"Oh, Jocelyn! Of course, I believe that. I knew Evelyn

almost as well as you did. I would never believe that of her. Not in a million years. Who said that?"

Jocelyn's cheeks flushed with renewed heat, her anger bubbling back up to the surface. "Inspector Ness! He came to my house to ask me some questions, and he said that when Evelyn was found, someone had written that word on a note left by her body. I tried to tell him that she had never been with a man, but he didn't believe me. He acted as though she was just very good at hiding her true nature."

"Inspector Ness said that?" Allison asked, obviously aghast.

Jocelyn nodded angrily. "I thought I could trust him. He'd done so much to help me find her. He..." She broke off, her face growing even hotter as she thought of the intimacies they'd shared.

"He... what?" Allison asked, her eyes narrowing shrewdly. "I didn't realize you and the inspector even knew each other."

"We don't," Jocelyn said, then lowered her gaze, unable to look her friend in the eyes. "At least, we didn't. I met him at your wedding breakfast, and when Evelyn went missing, I went to him for help."

"He's a good man," Allison said gently. "A bit stern, perhaps a bit hard around the edges. But I'm sure that he was just trying to do his job. He didn't know Evelyn like we did. He has to go in the direction where the evidence points."

"He hasn't been stern. Until last night, he was nothing but kind and helpful," Jocelyn told her friend in a rush. "That day we spent looking for Evelyn... I thought that we got to know each other quite well, and he... I let him kiss me." She couldn't yet tell her friend about what else she'd let him do. The mere thought of it still overwhelmed her with emotions she couldn't name.

"That's wonderful!" Allison cried, her eyes shining. "I'm glad that you felt attracted to him. You've always said you never felt desire for any man before."

"I was growing to trust him," Jocelyn admitted. "When he came to tell me what had happened... He held me very tenderly while I cried. I'd never had anyone offer me that kind of strength and understanding. I wanted..." She shook her head. "I don't know what I wanted. But when he came back to ask the questions, I was furious at his insinuations. Perhaps far more than I would have been had it been someone else saying such things. I just wanted so badly for him to believe me."

Allison reached across and squeezed her hand. "Of course you did."

"I told him to leave. I'm afraid I was quite nasty about it." She shook her head again as shame and embarrassment suddenly overwhelmed her. "I know he was just doing his job. I know he had to ask those questions... I hope that my unwillingness to cooperate with his line of questioning doesn't make it harder for him to find out who did this."

"I'm certain he understands that you're just upset... grieving... He's very professional. I know he'll somehow get to the bottom of this, whether you answer his questions or not. Quinn is still helping him, and the killer had to have made some mistakes this time."

"I hope so," Jocelyn said softly, realizing that she'd come here today more to talk about Sebastian than Evelyn. Her emotions were a tangled mess, and this was the very worst time for her to finally be feeling something for a man, but she couldn't deny that she did. She needed her friend to help her try to make sense of it.

"You really like him, don't you?" Allison squeezed her hand again. "It's all right if you do, Jocelyn. We can't do anything about what happened to Evelyn, but we can talk about what you're feeling for the inspector."

Maybe her friend was right. Did it cheapen her grief for Evelyn to admit that she was feeling something else as well? Was their any room for anything other than grief in her life right now?

Jocelyn released her rigid posture, allowing herself to sink back against the comfortable cushions of Allison's sofa. "I remember when you were staying with me, and you came home telling me all about the... things that you and Quinn saw when you went to that warehouse. The look in your eyes when you spoke of kissing him in that storeroom."

"And I remember your utter disgust. You said that you were so grateful you'd never have to let a man touch you again," Allison reminded her gently.

"It was terrible with Albert," Jocelyn admitted. "Even though it only went on for a few months until I became pregnant with Oliver, it seemed like hell on earth to have to endure that. The humiliation, the pain... I couldn't even imagine that anyone would ever enjoy those things. I didn't understand how you could seem so excited to be with Quinn. But when Sebastian kissed me..."

"It was different, wasn't it?"

"So different," Jocelyn agreed. "I could actually imagine that I might enjoy making him my lover." Surely, if her face got any hotter, she would simply explode. "I'm a widow," she said unnecessarily. "I could take a lover if I wanted to."

"You could," Allison said, nodding thoughtfully. "As long as you were discreet."

The ridiculousness of it all seemed insurmountable. "I can't believe I'm talking about this. There are so many other things I need to be doing right now. My sister isn't even in her grave yet, and I'm talking about taking a lover. What is wrong with me?"

"Nothing is wrong with you," Allison said sagely. "I think in times of despair, it's only natural to search for something happy, and lovemaking is the best way to celebrate life."

"Well, I don't know about that," Jocelyn said with a sigh. "But I'm glad you're not horrified by what I've told you."

"You're my best friend," Allison said with a tearful smile. "You could never say anything that would make me think less of you. Besides, you stuck by me when I was saying things much more horrifying than what you just said."

Jocelyn gave a half-laugh, half-sob, nodding. "Yes, and I even sat at a table with no place cards, so you know how much I love you."

They burst into tearful laughter and hugged each other tightly, and for the first time since she'd found out about Evelyn's death, Jocelyn felt like she could breathe again.

# Chapter Fourteen

The day of Lady Evelyn Lindsay's funeral dawned cold and dreary. Sebastian stood in front of the mirror in his parlor, fretting about his appearance for the first time in longer than he could remember. He hadn't worn this black suit in ages, not since he'd ridiculously observed a period of mourning after Marina's death, even though she'd left him years earlier and had died giving birth to another man's child. It seemed ill-fitting now and definitely looked like it was off-the-rack, which it was.

He straightened his tie and turned away with a mental shrug. It wasn't as though Jocelyn would even glance his way today. She had far too much on her mind, and she'd made it abundantly clear the last time he'd seen her that she wanted no more to do with him.

In fact, he'd thought long and hard about even going today. The last thing he wanted was to upset her further on what was already going to be an incredibly difficult day.

But throughout his many years of police work, he'd learned that killers liked to see the effect of what they'd done. There was a good chance that Evelyn's murderer would be at the graveside today, and he needed to use every bit of reasoning skill in his arsenal to figure out who it was.

When he arrived at the cemetery, he stood a bit apart from the rest, behind a huge oak tree, observing people as they arrived. His gaze immediately went to Jocelyn, who stood rigidly near the grave, a small, voluptuous figure in black. The lack of color emphasized her auburn hair even more, the tight chignon a bright splash of color against the gray sky.

She looked bereft, and he wanted nothing more than to race to her side and pull her into his arms once again. He wanted to be the port in her storm of grief, wanted to hold her and let her know that everything would be all right, that he would find who had done this to her sister and make him pay.

But he could guarantee none of those things, and she didn't want to talk to him anyway.

Forcing down his disappointment, he studied those around her. Quinn and Allison were there, of course. He knew that with her sister gone, Allison was the one Jocelyn would turn to for support.

Blackstone and his brother, Viscount Danbury, stood on the other side of Jocelyn. Blackstone looked very uncomfortable, fiddling with his cravat as though it were strangling him and staring at the stark hole where Evelyn's casket would be lowered. Danbury, on the other hand, who was a slimmer, less-intense version of his brother, looked as though he was perfectly at ease, occasionally touching Jocelyn's hand and bending his head to speak to her.

Sebastian had known that the brothers had grown up with Jocelyn and Evelyn, so their presence here today made perfect sense, but something seemed off about both of them. And he did not like the way that Danbury was being so solicitous toward Jocelyn.

For her part, Jocelyn didn't seem to like the attention she was getting from the viscount either. He saw her scoot a little closer to Allison several times, until O'Brien, who must have picked up on it as well, moved to her other side so that he and Allison made a shield around their friend.

Sebastian caught O'Brien's gaze and nodded grimly, and his friend gave a short nod in return. No doubt his former supervisor would have some insight for him on the viscount the next time they talked.

Two of Allison's three brothers were there. Lucien, the earl, and Morgan, one of the twins, along with their wives, Serenity and Fiona. Morgan was on Sebastian's list also, but of the seven names, he was the least likely suspect as far as Sebastian was concerned. That pained him, since Blackstone was on the list as well.

Now that he knew that one of the Strathmores was Prometheus, perhaps he should be even more suspicious, given his original theory that The Viper and Prometheus might be one and the same, but everything that O'Brien had said in the pub the other night made sense. Why would a man who devoted himself to rescuing children from lives of prostitution take to murdering young prostitutes? The Viper had obviously donned Prometheus's mask to throw them off his trail. He hated that it had worked, if only briefly. Besides, of the three brothers, Morgan seemed the least likely to be Prometheus.

O'Brien had said Strathmore was a kind and generous man who was devoted to his wife and children, and every interaction that Sebastian had with the man had convinced him of the same. Admittedly, he didn't know the man well though, so he watched him closely for several minutes.

However, nothing in the man's body language or mannerisms seemed to indicate that he was there for any reason other than to support a dear friend in her time of need. He seemed far more worried about his lovely redheaded wife's comfort, taking off his coat to wrap it around her shoulders despite her protests. Morgan and Fiona seemed very much in love, and once again, he thought how lucky in love Allison's family seemed to be.

He took out his small notebook, making notes about the other people in attendance. He recognized a few of the servants from Jocelyn's household—the nanny in particular seemed to be taking her mistress's death hard—but there were a few other aristocratic sorts that he didn't recognize. He made notes on their appearance so he could ask Quinn about them later.

Only one truly drew his interest, though. An older gentleman stood at the back of the cluster of those at the graveside, and his gaze occasionally bore into the back of Jocelyn's head, a look of pure hatred in his eyes. Sebastian found himself bristling on Jocelyn's behalf. Who was this gentleman, and why did he dislike Jocelyn so much?

The thought that this might be the killer, and that he might now have his eyes set on Jocelyn, sent a cold chill down his spine.

Skirting the crowd, he went to stand beside the man, reaching his side just as the minister began the ceremony. As the minister intoned the ancient words used to comfort those left behind, Sebastian tried to catalogue everything he could about the man for later reference. He stood a few inches shorter than Sebastian, and his balding gray hair must have once been blond. His crooked nose and protruding teeth made him appear ghoulish, the kind of old man who scared children.

When the ceremony finally came to an end, and those assembled were going up and throwing roses into the grave, Sebastian turned to the man, determined to find out what he knew. "Sad thing, this, isn't it?"

The man frowned and gave a shrug. "I didn't know the gel well."

That really didn't answer the question, did it? But the fact that the man's determination of whether this was a sad affair was based on how much it had impacted him seemed telling.

"How did you know Lady Evelyn?" Sebastian asked more directly.

The man gave Sebastian a once-over, his mouth turning down at his cheap suit and calloused hands. "Not that it's any of your business, but the girl's sister was married to my brother."

"I'm Inspector Ness from the Metropolitan Police," Sebastian offered. "I'm investigating Lady Evelyn's murder, so it rather *is* my business."

"Matthew Layton." The man gave a dramatic shudder. "The worst thing my brother ever did was marry that girl. I'm horrified that she's brought such shame on our old, distinguished name. Her sister murdered. Her name in the papers. I intend to give her a piece of my mind."

"It's hardly Lady Aston's fault that her sister was murdered," Sebastian snapped. It hadn't escaped him that this man's name started with an M, though he didn't believe he was a member of The Viper Club. He'd have to check the list again. "I'm guessing the reason that you're really angry at Lady Aston is because her child inherited your brother's title. You'd be sitting pretty right now if she hadn't have had a son, wouldn't you?"

"Well, I never!" Layton drew himself up, incensed, then whirled and stalked away.

Sebastian kept his eyes on the man until he got in his carriage and his driver drove away. If nothing else, at least Sebastian was glad that he'd saved Jocelyn from having to deal with that man today.

Of course, it made no sense that Layton would target Evelyn if Jocelyn was the source of his ire. Still, it wouldn't hurt to look into the man.

"What did you say to Layton?" O'Brien asked, coming up beside him.

"He was making noise about how Evelyn's murder had brought shame on his family name. I told him he was just mad that Jocelyn's son was the heir," Sebastian muttered.

O'Brien gave a quiet snort of laughter, and the two men walked a bit apart from the rest of the gathering. "Did you see anyone else acting suspiciously?"

Sebastian's gaze settled upon his superior. Though he wasn't quite ready to put into words his bad feeling about Blackstone, he couldn't shake the thought that something about the way he'd been handling the investigation so far did not make sense.

Quinn's gaze followed his, and he let out a deep sigh. "Yes. I thought the same."

"What should we do about it?" Sebastian asked.

"Just keep an eye on him. There's really nothing else we can do. He'd done nothing that warrants getting anyone else involved yet at least. I don't even think it's him. But I think he knows something." O'Brien looked as sick over the whole thing as Sebastian felt, and he knew his friend was far closer to

Blackstone than he was.

"What about the brother?" Sebastian asked quietly, still a little stung that the viscount seemed to be the one offering comfort to Jocelyn today when he wanted so badly for it to be him at her side.

"The families were close when they were young," O'Brien mused, a speculative look in his eyes. "Perhaps Evelyn rejected him in some way when they were growing up?"

"There may have even been an understanding of a match when they were older," Sebastian agreed. "If I can get Lady Aston to speak to me again, I'll try and find out what she knows about her sister's relationship with both of the Blackstones."

Quinn nodded. "Tread carefully, though, my friend. One misstep with the Blackstone family could easily cost you your career."

"I'm well aware," Sebastian said, frustration building within him. A killer walked among them, and his hands seemed to be tied. Even if The Viper wasn't one of the Blackstones, all the evidence pointed to the fact that it was someone like them, someone whose wealth and power made them all but untouchable.

Quinn clasped him on the shoulder. "Once you've spoken to Lady Aston, come by and see me. We'll go over everything from the newest case and see if we can get to the bottom of this, no matter where it takes us."

"I'll see you soon," Sebastian agreed as Allison joined her husband.

The lovely blonde met Sebastian's gaze, her blue eyes sparkling with intrigue. "I hear you've been spending time with

Lady Aston."

Heat rose in Sebastian's cheeks as he wondered what Jocelyn had told her friend. "I tried to help her find her sister."

Allison obviously knew a bit more of the truth than that, but she blessedly chose to keep that to herself. "She was a bit upset by your line of questioning the other day, but she's had some time to think it over and realizes that you were just trying to do your job. I think she's willing to speak to you now. Why don't you go pay your respects?"

Relief surged through him. "Thank you, Allison."

She nodded, then gave him an encouraging smile before she and Quinn turned toward their carriage. He stared after them for a moment, noting the way she took his friend's hand and leaned into him. Despite the seemingly insurmountable gulf of differences between them, they were making their marriage work.

Shaking his head, he turned away, his gaze immediately settling upon Jocelyn, who still stood by the graveside with the Blackstone brothers. Taking a deep breath, he headed in their direction.

"Inspector Ness." Blackstone gave him a stiff nod as he approached, looking less than thrilled to see him there. Again, the reaction did not make sense. For months, Blackstone had been railing at him to find out who The Viper was. Blackstone was certainly well aware of killers' tendencies to want to see the results of their crimes. He should be glad that Sebastian was here doing his job.

"Blackstone."

Blackstone cleared his throat. "You've met my brother, Viscount Danbury?"

"I don't think I've had the pleasure," Sebastian replied, turning toward the viscount, though all of his attention was centered on the beautiful, wan woman beside him. She looked as though she hadn't been sleeping, her eyes bruised and watery. "I'm Inspector Ness from J Division."

"You must be the one who's trying to catch The Viper," the viscount said enthusiastically. "Making any progress? It's a shame what's happening in our fair city."

Sebastian met the man's gaze, finding it hard to believe that this vapid, foppish-looking gent could either be the brutal killer he was looking for nor the brother of his hard-bitten, intense superior. How could these two men have been cut from the same cloth? "I believe I'm narrowing down my list," he said, letting the man make whatever he wanted of that. He turned to Jocelyn then, ignoring both the Blackstones. "May I speak with you a moment, Lady Aston?"

"I don't think this is the time or place," Blackstone cut in, glaring at Sebastian.

"Thank you, Drake," Jocelyn said softly. "But I don't mind. There are some things I'd like to say to the inspector."

Sebastian's heart warmed as Jocelyn turned away from the Blackstones and led him over toward the oak tree he'd been standing near earlier. He wondered if she'd seen him there.

"How are you, Jocelyn?" he asked softly, once they were out of earshot of anyone else.

Tears welled in her eyes, but she quickly blinked them away. "I am doing as well as can be expected, I suppose," she replied, her voice strained. "Today has been very hard."

He nodded, wanting so badly to once again take her in his arms. "I'm sorry that my questions the other day hurt you. That was never my intention."

"I know." She swiped at a tear that had escaped down her cheek, sniffling miserably. "You want to get to the bottom of this, and so do I. That doesn't mean it isn't difficult to hear the details of what happened to her. It hurt me when you didn't believe me when I told you that she did not sneak around with men."

"If you'll allow me to come and see you one more time, I promise that I will be very careful and respectful with the questions that I ask. But there are a few more things that only you would know the answer to."

"I'll do the best I can," she whispered.

"What time shall I come?" he asked.

A little hesitant, she said, "All morning, there will be people paying their respects, and there are so many reporters outside my front door at all hours of the day. I will come by your office tomorrow afternoon, if that's convenient."

"Thank you," he said, feeling as though she'd granted him a boon he was far from worthy of, even though he wished that she'd have allowed him to come to her house again. But he understood why she wanted to keep it professional. They'd crossed far too many lines already, and the reporters were still circling like buzzards, waiting for any chance of more salacious information. He could see a few now, kept at bay by common decency but still trying to get a scoop on what had happened. "I'll see you tomorrow afternoon then."

# Chapter Fifteen

Jocelyn watched Sebastian disappear through the trees, her gaze lingering on his broad shoulders, dark hair, and military bearing. She'd seen him the moment he'd arrived, and despite everything, her heart had leapt. He'd come! Even after she'd sent him away like a shrew, he'd still come here to be with her on one of the worst days of her life.

Of course, she knew that he was probably mostly here for his job, but she'd seen the sympathy and worry in his deep-blue eyes. She was almost certain that if there were not so many people watching them, he'd have taken her in his arms as he'd done before.

Dear Lord, how she wished he had. The strain of trying to be strong, to stand straight and not give in to her grief, was overwhelming. She would like nothing more than to collapse into Sebastian Ness's strong arms and give in to the fierce emotion inside of her.

But people were watching. In fact, she felt like the whole world was watching, gossiping and speculating about why The Viper had chosen Evelyn. What her sister had done to deserve this. She was tired of dodging reporters every time she left her house, tired of their shouts and suppositions. They were even here now, their cameras clicking and notebooks in hand.

She bit her lip until she thought it might bleed, then started back toward the gravesite, where a dozen or so people still milled around. Mortimer and Mandrake Blackstone met her halfway, and she tried to tamp down her irritation. Though she'd known the Blackstone brothers since she was a child, she hadn't seen them much as an adult, and she had no idea why they were both being so solicitous to her now. They were acting as though they were her brothers instead of family friends, and while she supposed she should appreciate that they were trying to comfort her, all she really wanted was to be left alone.

"Was he bothering you?" Drake asked darkly. "You really should have let me handle him, Jocelyn."

"He was fine," she said sharply. "I wanted to talk to him. Really, Drake, I should think you'd be happy to let him do his job."

"Men like that have no sense of what is right or proper," Mortimer cut in, shaking his dark head in disdain. "He had no right to be here, questioning his betters on such a tragic occasion."

"Men like what?" Jocelyn asked, letting some of her fury loose. "He's becoming a friend of mine, Mortimer. I'd suggest you mind your tongue. I am in no mood to listen to your elitist drivel." Even as she said the words, she was stunned by her daring. It was so unlike her to ever say what she was truly thinking. All her life, she'd been trained not to.

Perhaps Allison was wearing off on her, or perhaps she was starting to see that a man like Sebastian Ness was worth ten Mortimer Blackstones, despite his lack of pedigree and title.

Mortimer drew in a deep, offended breath, then spun around and walked away.

Drake watched him go, then sighed. "I'm sorry, Jocelyn. You're right. Ness is a good man, and my brother can be..." He shrugged. "Is there anything I can do for you before I leave? Anything you need?"

"No." She tried to smile but doubted it came very near the mark. She knew people were concerned about her, and that they were only trying to help, but was tired of everyone asking what they could do. "I appreciate your support, but I think only time will heal this loss."

She wasn't even certain that time would lessen the pain of losing Evelyn, but there certainly wasn't anything the Blackstones could do to help. All she wanted right now was to return home and fall into bed for the next twenty hours or so. Now that the funeral was over, maybe she could sleep at last. Perhaps she'd needed the finality of watching her sister's body lowered into the ground.

Blackstone squeezed her shoulder and then turned away, and Jocelyn's gaze met Abbie's. The nanny stood off to the side, her slim shoulders shaking as she grieved for her dearest friend. Realizing that Abbie was truly the only one who understood how great of a loss she'd suffered, she hurried to Abbie's side, embracing her tightly and finally giving in to her tears.

She caught a few shocked glances as she and Abbie clung together, but she didn't care what anyone thought about her grieving with the nanny. In fact, she wondered if she'd finally reached a point where she didn't care what anybody thought of her at all. Let the reporters snap their pictures and write their stories, let the members of the *ton* gossip. What did any of it matter now that Evelyn was gone?

THAT NIGHT, JOCELYN'S dreams were haunted. She was running through the park, trying to find Evelyn, but though she occasionally caught a glimpse of her sister's skirts disappearing through the trees, by the time she caught up, Evelyn was gone. Sobbing, she fell to her knees, only to be swept up into strong arms, cradled against a broad chest. She knew even before she looked up at his face that it was Sebastian. The terror that had filled her dissipated, replaced by intense desire.

She lifted her mouth to his, and he kissed her with hungry abandon, his tongue dancing with hers as his hands somehow both held her and caressed her. Then they were lying naked in the grass, their limbs intertwined as the kiss grew even more feverish, and once again, his fingertips delved between her thighs...

With a shuddering gasp, she awakened, bathed in sweat and tears, memories of the dream still so vivid she wasn't certain for a moment what was real.

Sebastian Ness had invaded every corner of her life during the last week. She couldn't get him out of her mind, and now she couldn't even escape him in her sleep.

Pushing out of bed, she drew on her robe, belted it, and padded over to the chair before the fire on shaky legs. Sinking into it, she reached out to the decanter of brandy on the nearby table and poured some into a crystal glass.

She didn't partake in spirits often, but she'd felt the need to have some handy ever since she'd learned of her sister's death. Taking a few sips, she let the warmth pool through her, chasing away the remnants of the dream.

Her thoughts drifted to the conversation she'd had with Allison about Sebastian. Rather than be shocked, her friend had seemed happy for her. She'd all but encouraged Jocelyn to have a dalliance with the man.

For the first time, she had to admit to herself how much she wanted him. These feelings of desire he inspired in her were too powerful to ignore. Even now, her body pulsed with something she couldn't even name, and the need to be in his arms again overwhelmed her.

Perhaps throwing herself into exploring these feelings could help stave off the grief and guilt that tormented her. Was that wrong? To want to choose life over death? To want to hide from what had happened to her sister for a while?

*I'm sorry, Evelyn. This doesn't mean I don't miss you, that you're not constantly in my thoughts. But I think you'd understand. I think you'd be happy that I finally found someone who makes me have butterflies, who makes me want to know what all the fuss is about.*

When he'd approached her at the funeral earlier, she'd told him she'd meet him at his office, but now she wished she'd told him to come to her home. But perhaps it was best to keep his questions separate from whatever else lay between them. His questions and his reaction to what she had to tell him about Evelyn might very well make her angry all over again.

With a sigh, she finished her glass of brandy, her thoughts racing with thoughts of tomorrow. When they were finished with the business side of things, did she have the courage to tell him that she wanted more?

# Chapter Sixteen

Sebastian hurried toward his office, his heart uncharacteristically racing with the knowledge that Jocelyn was waiting for him there. He'd been sure to keep himself busy elsewhere all afternoon, not wanting to appear too pathetically eager to see her, but that had meant that he'd been down in the dead room speaking to Dr. Lockwood when she arrived. Just because his main focus was The Viper didn't mean that murders didn't occur in Bethnal Green all the time. Now, he feared he'd kept her waiting for too long.

Shaking his head at himself, he stopped in front of his door, taking a deep breath and composing himself a bit before walking in.

"Good afternoon, Lady Aston," he murmured as he walked around his desk and took his chair facing her, though it felt a bit strange to once again be addressing her so formally after everything they'd shared. "I'm sorry to have kept you waiting."

"I understand," she murmured, staring at his desk as though unable to meet his gaze, her fair cheeks blushing. A tendril of her auburn hair had come loose from her neat chignon to drift along her jaw, and he wanted to tuck it behind her ear. "I know you're very busy."

"I'm never too busy for you," he said, the words slipping out before he could think better of them. He felt his own cheeks heat at the truth of them and was suddenly glad she wasn't looking at him. "I appreciate you coming down here. And I promise, I'll try my best not to upset you again."

She bit her lip and finally lifted her gaze. "I overreacted. I know you were just doing your job. I'll try not to take your questions so personally."

This was all so polite. He supposed he should be glad of that, but a part of him wanted to be anything but polite. He wanted to get back to the ease that had existed between them that first day they'd spent together. The jokes and sarcasm, the sexual tension and flirtation.

Clearing his throat, he shuffled a few piles of paper around needlessly, then grabbed a pencil and his little notebook that he took with him everywhere. "To your knowledge, did your sister ever turn down a marriage proposal?"

Her green eyes widened with surprise. That obviously hadn't been the question she was expecting. "There was always an understanding when we were children that she'd marry Mortimer Blackstone," she said, sending his heart racing for an entirely new reason. "But I don't think he ever actually asked her. Her first Season was not very successful, and I think Mortimer decided he could do better." She grimaced. "I never much cared for Mortimer, though I was quite close with Drake when I was younger."

"Why wasn't Evelyn's Season a success?" he asked gently. "She was a lovely girl. I'm sure she had a sizable dowry."

"Our dowries weren't as large as you might expect," she said quietly, flushing even more. "Our father had some problems with gambling. Lord Aston was willing to overlook that since he did not need my dowry and cared more about my breeding. But I imagine Mortimer thought differently."

"Do you think he was in need of a cash infusion?" he asked, his suspicions of his superior's brother growing.

She shrugged prettily. "Perhaps. But the other reason Evelyn's debut did not go as well as it could have was simply because she didn't try. She did not want to make a match, so she gladly became a wallflower. She did everything possible to make herself invisible to the men of the *ton*."

"She did not want to get married?" he asked, wondering why it surprised him so much. Of course, there were women who did not want to get married. He'd been married to one himself. Marina had never been suited to the life of a wife or mother. She seemed to have married him on a whim because that's what was expected of her, but she'd obviously regretted it almost immediately. Still, society left women, especially ladies, little other choice.

"She did not." Jocelyn sighed, shifting nervously in her seat. "I have something to tell you, something quite shocking. I'm willing to do so because I want you to be able to focus your attention in a different direction than trying to find out which men Evelyn was... in a relationship with. But if I do so, you have to promise me that what I tell you does not leave this office. It is for your information only, because I trust you, and I know you will not misuse the knowledge."

Intrigued, and humbled by her trust, he stood and went to the door, closing and locking it, trying to pretend he hadn't wanted to do so all along. He sat back down, giving her his full attention. "I promise I will keep whatever secret you choose to tell me. Your trust means the world to me, Jocelyn."

She stood and walked to the lone window, staring out at the street below. "I'm sure you are aware that there are people who... feel an attraction to those of their same sex?"

"Yes," he said very carefully, wondering where she was going with this. "I'm aware of that."

"Well, my sister Evelyn was one of those people. She was very in love with someone... just not a man. So I am absolutely certain that she was not what you said, that she did not have any secret lovers other than the one I am aware of. She was in love with my nanny, Abbie Morton. If you need to speak to her, she is willing to tell you whatever she knows. In fact, she is the one who told me I needed to tell you this. But if you do talk to her, just... be kind. She is grieving, too."

Sebastian sat back in his chair, stunned. Of course, he had heard of such things, but rarely among women and never among women of Evelyn's class.

It did not escape him that Abbie's surname began with the letter M, but of course, it was preposterous to even put her on the suspect list. The things that had been done to Evelyn were not what one woman would do to another.

Jocelyn remained by the window, her back stiffening more with each moment as she obviously waited for him to say something hurtful about the sister she'd loved so much. No wonder she'd been so convinced it was not one of her sister's lovers who'd killed her. He thought of the nanny at the funeral, the grief she'd done nothing to hide, and felt a wave of pity for the woman.

But maybe he was wrong. He'd known since his army days that there was no end to the horrors that one person could do to another. He had at least had to talk to Miss Morton before he ruled her out.

Pushing to his feet, he crossed the room in several long strides, knowing instinctively that Jocelyn needed to be held right now more than she needed any sort of platitudes. He pulled her back against him, and she sank into him with a little sob, turning in his arms and pressing her face against his chest.

"It's all right," he soothed. "I don't think any less of her. We can't choose who we love." The moment he said the words, he realized how true they were. His attraction and care for this lovely slip of a woman made absolutely no sense, but he couldn't fight it. He couldn't keep pretending it didn't exist.

How had his thoughts on the matter changed so drastically in such a short time? He could only suppose that he hadn't believed in love before because he'd never felt it. He'd always had a hard time taking things on faith. He'd seen too much ugliness to truly believe in the beauty he was experiencing with this woman.

"Thank you," she whispered. "I was so afraid to tell you. Afraid of what you might think. But they were so sweet together. If you'd known them, you'd understand that it was a good thing for both of them. I don't want it in the papers. I don't want people gossiping and turning it into something ugly."

"No one else has to know," he assured her. "I promise I'll keep this to myself."

"I know," she whispered with a shuddering sigh. "I do trust you, Sebastian. I'm sorry I told you to leave the other day. That was the last thing I truly wanted. The only time I feel all right is when I'm in your arms. I just haven't been thinking clearly—"

He cut her words off with a kiss. He couldn't help himself.

He wanted nothing more than to drown in the taste and feel of her. She moaned and wrapped her arms around his neck, kissing him back with an intensity he hadn't expected. Her passion ignited every inch of his body with a burning need that had to be quenched.

As he kissed her, he worked the tiny buttons that ran down the front of her gown, parting them impatiently until he was able to slide one hand inside her chemise and cup her full, luscious breast.

She gasped into his mouth, and for a moment, he thought she'd pull away. Instead, she lifted her hands and helped push the offending fabric away, baring herself to him more fully.

Breaking the kiss, he pulled back just enough to look at her, captivated by the erotic sight of her voluptuous breasts spilling out of the black muslin of her gown, her pale skin and rosy nipples such a contrast to his dark, callused hands.

"You are so lovely," he whispered, lifting his adoring gaze to hers, finding her eyes emerald pools of desire. He stroked her nipples with his fingertips, and she made a small, sensual sound of pleasure.

"That feels... so nice. I... I didn't know it could be like this." Her words made him feel as though he'd somehow won a very large prize, that he'd succeeded in something he hadn't even known was important. And he was determined to keep making her feel this way. The last thing he wanted was to disappoint her.

Bending his head, he took her nipple in his mouth, swirling his tongue around it until she cried out softly and buried her hands in his hair, holding him tighter against her.

Soon, he lavished the same attention on the other, while his free hand delved beneath her skirts, wanting to make her feel even better, wanting to give her the same pleasure he'd given her before.

He hooked her knee and placed her foot on a nearby box of paperwork, then ran his hand along her smooth calf, knee, then thigh. She gasped as he reached the springy thatch of hair at the juncture of her thighs, and he took her mouth once more with his as he traced the petals of her sex with his fingertips, finding her silky, hot, and damp.

Gently plumbing her depths with one fingertip, he used his thumb to seek out the sweet pearl of her desire, circling it until she was bucking and moaning against him, opening herself wider for his invasion. He worked her body with single-minded intent until she broke the kiss and cried out, shattering in his embrace.

He held her tightly, slowly removing his hand and placing her foot back on the floor as she tried to gather herself. He was rock-hard against her hip, his body thundering with the need to finally make her his, but this was not the time or place.

Now that he'd had a minute to think about it, he couldn't believe he'd done this at all, in his office of all places! Though he'd locked the door, anyone could have heard them. She certainly hadn't been quiet!

The memory of her passion, of her unbridled excitement, made him even harder, and he groaned, burying his face against the soft pillows of her breasts.

Her hands came hesitantly up to cradle his head against her, and her gentleness nearly unmanned him. His first instinct was to pull away, to deny that he needed this, but things between them were so fragile. The last thing he wanted was for her to think he was angry with her.

"That was incredible," she whispered at last. "That's twice now you've shown me that such pleasure was possible. But... I haven't done the same for you."

He laughed gruffly and finally eased away, tucking her back within her chemise with trembling hands. "Your pleasure gives me pleasure, darling." He began buttoning the impossibly tiny buttons. "I'm sorry that I did this here. I certainly didn't intend to, but there's something about you, something I just can't seem to resist."

She laughed hollowly. "I feel it, too, Sebastian. No matter how hard I try to, I can't get you out of my head."

"What do you think we should do about it?" he asked, knowing the answer should be nothing but wanting it to be so much more.

Her cheeks heated with embarrassment, but she held his gaze. "I would like to be alone with you. Do you think I could pay you a visit at your home?"

Her words thrilled and humbled him, though he was a bit embarrassed as well. "I live in a small flat. It's nothing like you're used to."

"I don't care," she assured him softly. "My position as a widow allows me some freedom... As long as I'm discreet, no one should care what I do. But I can't keep having you at my house. The servants will start to talk, and there are reporters everywhere. I don't want any more gossip, not after... what happened to Evelyn. My brother-in-law is already sniffing around, trying to find a reason to have me removed as Oliver's guardian. He would like nothing better than to get his hands on my son's inheritance. If he did, I'm sure there would be nothing left for Oliver when he reaches his majority."

Sebastian grimaced. "I had the misfortune of meeting the man at Evelyn's funeral. I'm afraid I angered him into leaving."

A laugh erupted out of Jocelyn, and she covered her mouth, flushing. "So, I have you to thank for that. I wondered where he'd gone. He's an odious little man. I knew he was there to stir up trouble."

"You're welcome," Sebastian said, his own lips curving into a smile. She was breathtaking when she smiled, and it was good to hear her laugh. He'd begun to fear she never would again.

Her smile faltered. "You must think me a trollop to make such an offer. A... whore."

He shook his head, hating to hear that word on her tongue, cupping her cheek gently. "I think you're the most amazing woman I've ever met. I'm humbled that you have any interest in me whatsoever. And whatever you decide, I promise that I will never tell another soul."

"I feel safe with you," she whispered. "No one else has ever made me feel safe."

Her words pierced him to the core, and he couldn't resist stealing another passionate kiss, hoping that he'd never do anything to make her regret them.

She finally pulled away, looking a bit dazed. "I should go. But if you'll write down your address, I'll come visit you tomorrow evening."

He nodded and went to his desk, hastily scrawling down his address. "When you come, can you bring Evelyn's diary? I'd like to read the whole thing, if you don't mind. She might have written something years ago that would help us find out who she might have rejected."

"Of course," Jocelyn agreed. "I will see you then."

He escorted her out to the lobby, for the first time glad that O'Brien no longer worked here, as the man would have been able to immediately see what had been going on between them in his office. As it was, his position as the inspector saved anyone from outright speculating. When Jocelyn came to him tomorrow, though, he'd have to tell her she shouldn't come to his office anymore. The last thing he wanted was to ruin her reputation in any way.

"Good day," he told her as she took her leave, wondering if she'd really go through with coming to his flat and dreading what a countess would think of the place if she did.

# Chapter Seventeen

As soon as Jocelyn left the police station, she was assailed with doubts. What had she done? She couldn't believe she'd come here today with the intention of propositioning him in such a way. She'd become a person that she didn't even recognize, and she didn't know whether that thrilled or terrified her.

She sank back into the comfortable cushions of her coach in a very unladylike slouch, her heart racing as she thought about the deliciously wicked things she and Sebastian had done in his office. Even now, just the thought was enough to send little shivers throughout her body. Every time he touched her, she understood more clearly why Allison had risked so much to be in Inspector O'Brien's arms. If he'd made her feel even a tenth of what Sebastian made Jocelyn feel, it suddenly all made sense.

The thoughts of what had just transpired kept her mind busy nearly all the way across town, but as her carriage lumbered through Mayfair, thoughts of Evelyn took control once more.

Sebastian seemed certain that Evelyn's killer had been someone she'd rejected, and she began to wonder whether her sister *had* rejected Mortimer Blackstone. She'd like to believe that Evelyn would have told her, but it would have been years ago, probably around the time of her sister's eighteenth birthday.

Jocelyn had still been just a girl, so maybe Evelyn hadn't yet felt that she could confide such a thing to her. She might also have still been struggling with the fact that she did not want to ever be in a relationship with a man. Perhaps she'd been frightened and confused by her own feelings.

If Evelyn had rejected Mortimer, he probably wouldn't have made that public. But she could see how it would have hurt his pride. Had he been letting that fester within him all these years?

More importantly, did a man like that have it within him to do such a horrific thing to another human being? She'd always thought of Mortimer as a weak-willed dandy.

Shivering for an entirely different reason, she waited for her footman to open the carriage door as they pulled up in front of her house.

Once inside, she found herself drawn to Evelyn's room. She wandered around for a while, her fingers skimming over her sister's things, still finding it hard to believe that Evelyn would never return. She'd never again wear her favorite scarf or reread any of her favorite books. She'd never again write the small occurrences of her life in her diary.

With a sob, she sank down on Evelyn's bed, burying her face in the pillow that still vaguely smelled of her sister's subtle rose-scented perfume. She'd been fine most of the day, but here, surrounded by her sister's things, she couldn't pretend that everything was okay, that Evelyn was simply at the library, the park, or one of her meetings.

A FEW HOURS AFTER JOCELYN had left, Sebastian looked up as Constable Pond led Miss Morton into his office. He was a bit surprised that the constable had managed to bring her in so quickly.

"Miss Morton," he said, gesturing for her to have a seat and nodding his gratitude at the young constable, who flushed at the unspoken praise and shut the door behind him.

"Inspector Ness," Miss Morton replied, taking a seat and staring at him with red-rimmed eyes.

"Thank you for coming down," Sebastian said, his pity for the girl growing as he took in her absolutely devastated mien. "I know this is a difficult time for you."

He couldn't imagine how hard it must be to love someone, yet have to hide it.

Or maybe he could.

She simply nodded, her dark eyes pooling with tears. "Lady Aston told you... About me and Evelyn?"

"Yes." Sebastian handed her his handkerchief. "I'm glad you came forward. It couldn't have been easy, but you've saved me a lot of fruitless investigation."

Miss Morton nodded jerkily, dabbing at her eyes. "I w-want to help you catch the... m-monster who did this."

If she'd had anything to do with Lady Evelyn's death, she was a magnificent actress.

He cleared his throat and reached for his notebook. "Can you tell me what you know about the man who was harassing Lady Evelyn? The one she'd rejected but wouldn't leave her alone?"

The puzzlement on Miss Morton's face didn't seem feigned. "Evelyn never said anything about such a man."

The hope he'd had going into the conversation fizzled into frustration. Who was Miss Morton trying to protect? If Evelyn had talked to Heather Fields about the man who'd been bothering her, surely she'd spoken to the woman she loved about it as well.

He sighed. "Miss Morton... Please... You have to tell me everything you know."

She shook her head, crying even harder now. "Evelyn would never have told me about something that was troubling her. She always tried to protect me. She didn't want to worry me. That was one of the only things we ever fought over."

His eyes narrowed. "Did you fight a lot?"

"No!" she said on a sob. "Hardly ever. We were very happy together. She's the only one who ever truly loved me."

Miss Morton buried her face in her hands, and he knew he'd gotten everything out of her he was going to. She'd loved Lady Evelyn Lindsay, and Evelyn had apparently loved her enough to shield her from anything ugly that was going on in her life.

Since they'd never leaked the information that The Viper put the word *whore* near his victims, it was safe to say that Evelyn's murderer and the one who'd killed the Mercy House girls were one and the same. Looking at fragile, broken little Miss Morton, he couldn't imagine that she'd had the strength nor intent to commit these crimes. She was exactly what she appeared, a grieving loved one.

"I'm sorry to have upset you," he said, feeling like an ass. "I appreciate you coming down here today, but I think I have everything I need from you. You're free to go."

She blinked up at him, her dark eyes luminous pools of pain. "Promise me you'll catch him. Promise you'll make him pay."

He swallowed, wishing she hadn't asked this of him, wishing he didn't have one more person depending on him to make things right. "I'll do my best," he said, hoping his best was good enough.

SEBASTIAN SPENT THE rest of the day trying to find out everything he could about the Blackstone brothers, all without alerting anyone else that he was looking into them. This was somewhat difficult to do, given that they were aristocrats and one was his immediate supervisor.

The only one he felt he could trust with this information was O'Brien, and since Quinn didn't even officially work for the police anymore, there wasn't much his friend could do.

As the day had worn on, he'd become more and more convinced that one of the Blackstones was The Viper. Though a fat lot of good that knowledge did him. There was no way he could prove it, and coming forward with his theory would almost certainly cost him his job, which wouldn't help Jocelyn or Miss Morton at all.

At the end of the day, reluctant to go back to his empty flat and obsess over the fact that tomorrow night he might not be alone there, he made his way to O'Brien's house in Belgravia.

The butler showed him into O'Brien's office, and as he waited for his friend, Sebastian strode across the room to the wall that was full of their wildest theories and guesses about

The Viper's identity. Never once had they guessed it might be the assistant commissioner or his brother.

Sebastian wasn't certain which would hurt him more, that Blackstone was the killer or that he knew it was his brother and had been covering for him this whole time.

Had Blackstone promoted Sebastian just so he could see whether he or his brother were under suspicion? His stomach churned at the thought that perhaps he'd been made inspector not because he was the best man for the job but because he was the worst. Did Blackstone think that Sebastian would never solve the murders? What better way to avoid getting caught than to control the investigation?

"Ness!" O'Brien said as he entered the room. "I wasn't expecting you tonight."

"I'm sorry for dropping by unannounced," Sebastian said, turning around and shaking O'Brien's hand. "But everything I've learned since the funeral has pointed toward one of the Blackstones, and there's no one else I can talk to about it."

O'Brien frowned and went to shut the door. "I've been afraid of that myself."

With a sigh, Sebastian caught his friend up on all that had happened after the funeral and what he'd learned from Jocelyn. "So you see my dilemma," he finished.

O'Brien nodded grimly. "My money's on Danbury. I've never cared for the man. Something about him has always set my teeth on edge." He strode back over to the wall and looked at their prior work on the case for what Sebastian was certain must be the thousandth time. "After Polly Keys' murder, he walked into my office while Blackstone and I were discussing it. He asked about how the case was progressing with a sick sort of glee."

"I think it's him, too. I'm just not certain if Blackstone knows. Is that why he's been acting so erratically? Ordering me not to interview Lady Aston? Is he protecting the sick bastard?"

O'Brien sighed grimly and took his seat behind his desk, waving Sebastian toward the other chair. "I hope not. That would cost him his career, and I've always liked the bloke."

"As do I," Sebastian agreed. "But if he's known of his brother's activities this whole time and done nothing to stop him, I think he should lose more than his job. He might have been able to save Evelyn's life."

Drumming his fingers restlessly on the desk, O'Brien nodded. "I hate to think this of him, though. I've always thought he was one of the few in his position who was actually trustworthy and moral. Perhaps he's been acting so strangely because he suspects his brother but isn't certain? This isn't the sort of thing you'd accuse your own brother of if you weren't sure. Maybe he's been running his own investigation into the matter?"

"I hope so," Sebastian said with a sigh. As an only child himself, he had no real idea of the lengths one might go to help a sibling. "But it's counterintuitive to be working against us this way."

"So, what do you want to do about it?" Quinn asked, raising a brow.

"What can I do?" Sebastian groused. "I've been looking into both of the Blackstones, but there's not much I can find out without alerting them that I'm doing it. And I'm not certain enough that one of them is The Viper to ruin my whole career."

"I'll start looking into them as well," O'Brien said. "My brothers-in-law might know something. They run in the same circles and might have heard if there were any rumors or gossip about them."

"Do what you can," Sebastian said with a nod. "I really appreciate all your help on this."

"I want to catch this bastard, too," O'Brien replied with quiet intensity. "He crippled me for life, made me quit the job I loved, and killed women under my wife's care. I have a thousand reasons for wanting to stop him."

"We have to figure this out," Sebastian agreed. "I don't think I could live with myself if this bastard kills anyone else under my watch."

O'Brien sighed and turned back toward the wall of photos and notes. "I'm interested in the lock that was found on the gardener's shed. It's better quality than the one that was there originally. So our man breaks open the original one but brings along one of his own. He could have just broken the lock and left the door open, but he obviously wanted to buy himself some time. Slow us down so that we wouldn't find Evelyn's body right away. I thought we could start investigating shops that sell high-quality locks. See if anyone remembers selling one like the one we found to any of the men on our list."

"Well, it's not much to go on, but at least it's something. At least it gives me something to do." Sebastian came to join his friend at the wall, hoping against hope that this time, he'd see something he hadn't seen before. That somehow, all the pieces of the puzzle would slide into place.

"I wonder how Lady Evelyn received the note asking her to

meet him at the park and what happened to it?" Quinn mused.

"That's a good question. It doesn't seem like the killer would have been brazen enough to deliver it to her house, nor that she'd have run into him at one of her meetings. So how did she get it?"

He and Quinn passed ideas back and forth for another hour before Sebastian finally decided to call it a day. He needed to get home and bathe, straighten his rooms, and hope that Jocelyn didn't come to her senses.

Or maybe he should hope that she did because he had a very bad feeling that once he'd made love to her, it would be even more difficult for him when she inevitably walked away.

# Chapter Eighteen

Jocelyn alighted from her carriage in front of the address Sebastian had given her, her gaze darting nervously around the Bethnal Green neighborhood where he lived. He'd told her that his flat was not what she was used to, but somehow, she'd still expected that a police inspector would have better lodgings than these.

"Are you certain this is the correct address, my lady?" the footman, Thomas, asked her quietly. "I don't feel right about leaving you in this neighborhood overnight."

She'd told Thomas and her driver that she was going to visit a friend for the evening, though she was pretty sure they already knew exactly what she was really planning. She trusted their discretion, but who knew what they would do if they truly thought she was in danger?

Taking a deep breath, she met the footman's worried gaze. "My friend is Inspector Ness," she admitted. "I'll be fine."

Thomas's eyes widened, and he gave a jerky nod. "Of course, my lady. But I'll escort you up, and we'll make certain he's home."

"Thank you," she said, feeling relieved. She'd been quite nervous about trying to navigate the large brick building where his flat was located all by herself.

Thomas took the small valise she'd brought, and she followed him into the dim interior. Inside, the mingled scents of old cooking, sweat, and, heaven help her, *urine* lingered unpleasantly. She rushed to keep up with the footman's long-legged stride as they mounted some steep stairs up to the second floor.

"Here we are, my lady," the footman announced, rapping on the correct door.

Almost immediately, Sebastian opened it, a welcoming smile on his handsome face. "Good evening," he greeted her, his blue eyes filled with such dark promise that it took her breath away. "I wasn't certain you'd come."

She turned to her footman. "Pick me up at nine in the morning," she instructed him. "And please, don't tell anyone where I am."

Thomas nodded and gave her the ghost of a smile. "Have a good night, my lady,"

The moment Thomas turned to walk back down the hall, Sebastian pulled her into the safety of his flat, locking the door behind her. "All day, I was certain that you'd come to your senses."

"I think I've lost complete control of my senses," she said with a small helpless laugh. "Perhaps it's even worse than that. Perhaps I've lost my faculties completely."

He shook his head, tugging her toward a well-worn sofa in front of a fireplace, where flames crackled merrily. "I think for once in your life, you're doing exactly what you want to do."

Maybe he was right. Even though it seemed wrong on so many levels, she couldn't deny the excitement surging through her. She had no idea what the night would bring, but she had a feeling she was going to enjoy it immensely.

When she was seated, he hovered anxiously above her. "Can I get you anything? You must be freezing from your trip over."

She shrugged out of her coat, trying to smile, even though she was indeed shivering. The February chill had cut through her like a knife. "What I'd really like is for you to sit down here with me. I always feel warm in your arms."

He sank down beside her, wrapping one arm around her shoulders and pulling her snugly against him. "I still can't believe you're really here."

She sighed, resting her head on his chest. "I couldn't stay away."

"You're staying the whole night?" He nudged her bag.

"Is that all right?" she asked, suddenly wondering if she'd presumed too much. What if he didn't want her there all night?

"Of course, it's all right," he assured her. "It's more than all right. I love the thought of waking up with you in the morning."

She flushed and buried her face against his broad chest. "I don't know how these things are done. I've never—"

"I know," he said quickly. "I know, and I'm glad to answer any questions you might have."

She bit her lip, but knew no matter how embarrassing it might be, she had to ask a very important question. "How do we keep from... having a baby?" She knew very little about these matters, but the one thing she did know from experience was the end result.

"I'll do my best to keep you safe," he assured her. "But

there's no guarantee that it won't still happen."

"Oh," she whispered, feeling as though a bucket of water had been dashed upon her head.

"Do you remember when you were with your husband... when he released inside you?"

She nodded jerkily. "Yes, but I'd rather I didn't."

His lips quirked in a smile. "Well, if we keep that from happening, if I pull out at the last minute, you should be fine." He held her gaze. "But it's not completely effective. It's all right if you don't want to take that risk. I won't be angry. There are other things we can do... Other pleasures we can explore."

She gulped, both fascinated and terrified by the thought of what those pleasures he spoke of might be.

He hugged her tighter. "You don't have to decide anything this moment. Let's just sit here and enjoy each other's company for a while, shall we?"

She nodded jerkily. "Yes, let's do that."

For a long moment, they sat silently side by side as the fire crackled merrily in front of them. Some of the chill that had sunk into her bones on the way over gradually began to dissipate, and she relaxed into him, so grateful for his patience and understanding.

She'd never had a friend like him. Someone who made her feel both safe and excited. Cared for yet desired. Though she'd only known him a short time, she was already having trouble imagining her life without him.

"How are you doing?" he asked her quietly after a long time. "Do you want to talk about it... about your sister?"

"I have been doing better the last few days," she told him, surprised to realize it was true. "I'm still sad... I still miss her every day... But the bottomless grief is dissipating. What I mostly feel now is anger. I'm absolutely furious at the thought that someone took her from me. Even more so that it might be someone I know and trust."

"I'm angry, too," he replied, his blue eyes burning into hers. "I'm angry that this monster is taking these women, one at a time, right beneath my nose, and so far I've been unable to stop him."

She supposed that would be a very heavy burden to bear. But she didn't put any of the blame on him. How could he have ever guessed that The Viper would so quickly move on from Bethnal Green prostitutes to a refined lady of the *ton*?

Suddenly remembering that she'd brought Evelyn's diary, she pulled it out of her coat pocket and handed it to him. "I hope this will help. I wanted to look through it myself, but I just couldn't bring myself to do so. Reading her words was like hearing her voice in my head. It was just too hard." Her throat thickened, and she swallowed painfully.

Sebastian took the small, leatherbound book from her almost reverently. "Thank you. Hopefully, there's something in here that can help us."

"I'd like it back when you're done with it," she said unnecessarily. "Perhaps in time, I'll have the strength to read it."

He squeezed her hand. "I'm certain of it. You are stronger than you know, Jocelyn."

Once again, she wondered at her daring in coming here. She'd been the sensible, responsible one her entire life. She'd always followed the rules, even when they didn't make sense to her.

And where had it gotten her?

An empty, lonely life with only her son, sister, and one friend to comfort her.

But Evelyn's death had taught her that time was not guaranteed. If she didn't live for today, there was no guarantee that she'd still be here tomorrow. If she didn't explore the passion between them tonight, there was no guarantee that she would ever have this opportunity again.

"You've awakened something in me I never dreamed I could feel," she whispered. "I think I'm ready now to begin to explore it. But I need you to teach me. I'm woefully ignorant about what truly happens between a man and woman."

He caught his breath, his eyes flaring with desire. "I would love to be your teacher. But first, I just need to be certain that you want this as much as I do. That you're not just doing this out of fear and loneliness."

She shook her head, allowing a small, helpless laugh. "I don't know, Sebastian. I really don't know. I never would have thought of doing this just a few weeks ago. But I'm here now, and no matter what my reasons are, I want to be. I want *you*."

"I want you, too," he replied, right before his lips captured hers.

She melted against him, glad that he seemed to be done asking questions. She didn't want to talk about any of it anymore. She just wanted to feel.

He didn't disappoint. Within seconds, the passion that always simmered between them had ignited into a bonfire of need and exploration. She'd never known a kiss could be so all-consuming.

Finally, he broke away, gasping. "I want to see you," he breathed. "This time, I want to be able to take my time, explore your lovely body from head to toes."

The thought of being naked in front of him, of baring herself completely to his touch and gaze, was terrifying. What if he didn't like what he saw?

"I've had a baby," she managed to get out. "My body is probably not what you're used to."

"Oh, Jocelyn..." He pressed a hot kiss to her throat. "I could never be displeased by anything about you. You're beautiful, inside and out."

Warmed by his words, she summoned every ounce of courage she possessed and pushed to her feet. If he wasn't bothered by a little extra padding and some stretch marks, why should she be? Those things had been the price of her son, and she'd gladly pay it again.

He stood as well, moving her hair aside to get to the tiny buttons that ran down her back. "You have the most gorgeous hair," he said, his breath hot against the back of her neck as he worked. "I've thought so since the first time I saw you."

Most people thought her hair was too... much. Too bright. Too different. She loved that he loved it.

The dress suddenly sagged as the buttons were released, and she grasped the front of it, holding it against her breasts. "I'd like to see you, too," she told him daringly. "If I must bare myself to you, I think it's only fair you do the same."

He smiled and nodded. "You're absolutely right. It's only fair."

Keeping her gaze on him, she slowly began to undress, shrugging off the heavy gown, then all the other layers that women were made to wear. For his part, Sebastian took off his coat and vest, then his white shirt, leaving his powerful chest bare.

Never before had she seen a man like this. Even her husband had come to her in his night shirt. Sebastian's bare chest was a symphony of muscle and smooth, taut skin. He looked like a Greek statue, and it took her a moment to realize she'd stopped what she was doing entirely, so engrossed was she at the sight of him.

He cleared his throat gently, his hands on his belt, and she only began again because she wanted to see the rest of him. She wanted it very much.

Undoing his belt, he pushed his trousers down until they puddled on the floor, and all that remained were a pair of clean but worn drawers. Jocelyn realized she had never seen a man's undergarments, not even in a haberdashery. She'd assumed that men wore an all-in-one suit like the little ones Oliver wore, but Sebastian's were like a second skin of trousers. The thin white linen fabric clung to him, with a straining line of mother-of-pearl buttons down the front holding back a very prominent arousal that she was certain hadn't been there when they'd stood up.

She let her chemise drop just as he took off that last barrier as well, and suddenly, they stood before each other as naked as the day they'd been born.

His... she didn't even know what to call that part of him... stood rigidly at attention, larger than she'd imagined, given her memory of what had transpired between her and the earl. Did they come in different sizes?

"You're absolutely beautiful," he breathed, taking a step closer.

She shivered, crossing her arms over her chest. "So are you."

"Are you cold?" he asked, grabbing a blanket off the back of the couch and wrapping it loosely around her.

The small room was actually pleasantly warm, in a way that the larger rooms of her home rarely were. However, it wasn't the cold that had made her shiver, but the sight of him, so virile and powerful. His stark male beauty both exhilarated and terrified her.

"Thank you," she murmured, finally lifting her gaze from his body to his face. "I'm fine. I'm just... afraid. I've never been completely naked in front of anyone except my lady's maid."

Taking her hands, he pulled her back to sit on the couch. "We don't have to do anything you don't want to do," he reiterated. "The last thing I want to do is frighten you."

"When Allison met Mr. O'Brien, they saw... a sex act being performed in a warehouse. She came home that evening so excited and intrigued by it, wanting to talk about it. I'm afraid I was not at all willing to do so. I hated everything about having... relations with Albert. I couldn't understand why she would willingly want to do such a thing, for the pleasure of it, not just as a necessary chore to conceive a child." She wasn't even certain where she was trying to go with this, just wanted to let him know how much this all frightened her, how badly her marriage had scarred her.

He grimaced. "I wish your husband had taken better care of you. It pains me to think that it was so awful for you. It shouldn't have been. He should have taken his time and been gentle with you."

"It wasn't just that he was rough... that he hurt me..." She swallowed and shook her head. "He treated me as though I was just a possession, that my body was his to do whatever he wanted with."

He cupped her bare shoulder beneath the blanket, squeezing gently. "I don't want to own you, Jocelyn. I only want to make you feel good."

"And you have," she whispered. He'd given her pleasure twice without taking any in return. She suddenly wanted to rectify that. "Now, I'd like to do the same for you. It occurs to me that maybe if I... touch you, if I learn about your body the way you've learned about mine, that maybe I won't be so afraid of it."

His blue eyes dilated with passion, and he leaned forward to kiss her on the tip of the nose. "If that's what you want, darling, I am more than happy to accommodate you. Wait here for just a few minutes. I want you to be as comfortable as you can be."

Standing, he strode down the hall, and her gaze caught hungrily on his slim, muscular backside. It didn't seem to bother him at all to walk around naked, and she suddenly wished for the same sort of confidence. It would be so freeing.

Before she could even wonder too much about what he was doing, he returned with his arms full of blankets and pillows. She assumed he'd retrieved them from his bedroom.

"It's cold in the bedroom," he told her, as he knelt before the merry little fire and spread them out before it. "I thought you might like to stay in here."

"Thank you." She nodded, pleased by his thoughtfulness. Already, he was exceeding expectations.

After a few minutes, he'd made a comfortable little nest for them, and he reclined back on the pillows, patting the space beside him that was even nearer to the fire. "Come lay with me,

Jocelyn."

She shivered, though not at all from the cold. The heat in his voice did strange things to her.

Wrapping the blanket around her shoulders around her more fully, she stood and crossed to his side, sinking down beside him. He was lying on his side, his head propped up with one arm, his beautiful body completely bare to her interested gaze. He was as unlike Albert as he possibly could be, and her fingertips ached to touch him, to run her hands over all that taut, smooth skin.

"I don't know how to do this," she whispered. "I assume that there is a way that I can please you, as you did me, that does not actually involve... you inside me?"

"There is," he murmured, his voice husky, that part of him seeming to swell even more. "I'll show you. But please tell me if you don't feel comfortable, if you want to stop. I want you to enjoy this as much as I know I will."

His words gave her peace of mind, and the last of her reservations fell away. "I will," she assured him.

Tentatively, she placed her hand on the center of his chest. His skin was warm and as smooth as it looked. She met and held his gaze, a wave of intense tenderness washing through her. "I can feel your heart beating, Sebastian."

He smiled ruefully, and he placed his hand over hers, squeezing gently. "It's very intimate, to be with someone like this."

She bit her lip and nodded. "Show me how you want to be touched. Show me what I should do."

Still holding her gaze, he moved her hand slowly down the muscles that lined his stomach, and she gasped at the sensation of the silky line of hair that seemed to point the way to his straining arousal against her fingertips.

"What should I call it?" she asked.

He smiled at that. "My cock. Dick. Manhood. Knob. Pud. Wick. Twig. There are dozens of names for it. What do you like the most?"

She swallowed thickly, wondering if she had the courage to say such a dirty word. "Cock," she breathed, just as their hands reached it. "I like that one the most."

Hot. Silky. Smooth. It didn't feel anything like she'd thought it would.

"Wrap your hand around it," he said, his voice rough.

She did as he'd asked, feeling wonderfully wanton and daring. "Like this?"

He nodded jerkily, then closed his hand around hers again, showing her how to stroke up and down. When she'd gotten the idea of it, he released her, and she continued, watching his face as she did so. It made her feel remarkably powerful to see his handsome face go taut and strained, his eyes closed, his neck arched. And she found that she liked the feeling of him in her hand, the hardness she knew was because he was aroused.

"You're a fast learner," he said after a few minutes. "I love the feel of your hands on me, Jocelyn. I feel like I've been waiting a lifetime for this."

"I like it, too," she replied, her voice so sultry she hardly recognized it. "I like having your cock in my hand."

"Christ," he hissed, and she realized he'd liked it when she'd said that dirty word. He'd liked it very much.

"Don't stop," he growled, reaching up with one hand and pulling her head down to his, kissing her ferociously as she continued to stroke him. His mouth was hot and sweet, tasting of bourbon and something she could only describe as Sebastian.

*My lover...*

The words had such a strange power for her, and she repeated them over and over in her mind as she kissed him wildly, striving to give him the same pleasure he'd given her.

*My lover. My lover. My Sebastian.*

And she realized he'd been telling the truth when he'd said that giving her pleasure had pleased him as well. How could she not love knowing that she was making him feel good, that she was capable of doing this for him, despite her inexperience?

Finally, he broke the kiss and cried out, his big body jerking as his cock sent a hot white liquid cascading into her hand.

She sank back, a bit stunned, suddenly realizing that this was what he'd said he couldn't do inside her. This was his seed, what caused babies, and she was holding it in her hand. She couldn't believe that she'd been married for nearly two years, had given birth, and she was only now understanding the mechanics of it.

"Are you all right?" she asked tentatively.

He opened his eyes and smiled, and the beauty of it, of this handsome man she was starting to care far too much for, touched her to the core.

"I'm better than all right," he said huskily. "It had just been a long time for me, and it felt so good I wanted to savor it for a moment."

"Oh," she said, her face heating with embarrassed happiness. *I made him feel good.*

Seeing how awkwardly she was holding his seed, he

stretched back toward the sofa and grabbed his shirt, using it to clean off her hand in a such a matter-of-fact way that she couldn't be embarrassed about it.

Once he was done, he drew her back down beside him, cuddling her against the warmth of his naked body. This was perhaps the most fantastic thing yet, to be pressed up against him, skin against skin, an intimacy unlike anything she'd ever known.

"Are you warm enough?" he asked softly, brushing his lips against her forehead.

"Yes," she murmured. The crackling fire kept her backside toasty warm, and her front was even warmer from the heat of his big body. "I've never been naked for so long, just out in the open like this. I'm usually only naked in the bath and then just for brief moments as I change from one garment into another. It feels wonderfully freeing."

He laughed softly. "I rarely am either. Perhaps it's the soldier and the policeman in me, but I usually don't like being vulnerable like this. I stay fully dressed unless I'm in bed. And even then, I wear nightclothes. I suppose I want to be ready for the worst at all times. But I don't mind being naked with you. It feels comfortable."

She smiled against his chest, liking the fact that they were so close he could probably feel it. "Then let's be naked as much as possible during our times together."

His arms tightened around her. "Does that mean you want to do this again?"

"Of course," she said. "I love being with you, Sebastian. I want us to be lovers." Again, her face grew hot at her own daring, and she was glad he couldn't see it. She couldn't believe she'd actually asked for what she wanted. Had she ever done such a thing in her entire life? What was it about this man that made her feel so free to be herself?

With a swiftness that made her a little dizzy, he rolled her so she was on her back and he was on his side looking down at her, his handsome face serious, but a gleam of happiness in his beautiful blue eyes. "Are you certain? You're a countess, and I'm a lowly police inspector. I can't get over feeling as though I'm not good enough to kiss your dainty little shoes, let alone all the things I want to do to other parts of you."

"It doesn't matter," she assured him. "It's not like we're getting married. No one ever has to know about this."

He stiffened, and she immediately knew she'd said the wrong thing. When she played it back in her mind, she cringed. "I didn't mean it like that," she hastened to assure him. "I wouldn't care if the whole world knew about it. You're more than good enough for me, Sebastian. I just like the idea of you being my lover. To have this one beautiful thing that is just for me, for my pleasure. That in this one part of my life, I don't have to worry about all the rules."

He nodded, looking as though her words had somewhat appeased him, though she suspected that deep down, he was still hurt, which was the last thing she'd wanted.

"Well, if this is all I can be for you, then I feel as though I have to make it my duty to be the very best lover I can be," he told her, letting his hand drift from her face, down the column of her throat, then cupping one of her breasts and toying with her nipple. "Are you ready for more?"

"Yes," she breathed. "I want to know what it's like to truly make love to you, Sebastian. I want to know how it feels to have you inside me."

He gave a low, sexy growl of a sound and captured her mouth with his. At her hip, where his cock had gone soft, she felt it begin to harden once more. As they kissed passionately, his hands roamed her body, tantalizing her breasts and between her thighs until she was gasping and moaning into his mouth, trying to again know that feeling he'd given her once before.

At last, he rolled on top of her, bracing his arms on either side of her head to keep his weight from crushing her. He broke the kiss and stared down into her eyes, spreading her thighs with his own and then settling between them so she could feel his hardness pressed against her damp, aching sex.

"Tell me again that you want this," he demanded, his voice a low, husky growl. "Tell me you want me."

"I want you," she said, hoping he knew how much she meant it, not just at this moment but all the time. "I want you inside me, Sebastian."

"I love hearing you say that." Reaching between them, he took himself in hand and rubbed the tip against her, teasing and tantalizing her until she didn't think she could stand it any longer.

Seeming to know when she'd reached her limit, he thrust into her in one smooth stroke, then stayed deep within her, his arms trembling as he stared down at her. "Is that all right? Does it feel good? I don't want to hurt you."

She bit her lip, the pleasant fullness like nothing she'd experienced with Albert. She knew now that her husband had never taken the time to prepare her, to make sure her body was ready for him. With Sebastian, there was no pain at all, just him and her, linked together. For this moment at least, they were one.

"It's good," she breathed. "So good."

"For me, too," he said, and then he began to move. Any coherent thought she'd ever had fled in the wake of the pleasure that surged through her. Then he put his hand between them, once more toying with the spot she hadn't even known about, and the combined sensations were indescribable.

Within a few minutes, she was pulsing around him, crying out in pleasure as he continued to thrust deep within her. She realized she was crying, not from sadness or anger this time, but from the sheer beauty of it.

Then he stiffened and jerked away from her, spilling his seed on her stomach before he collapsed on his side next to her.

She reached for his shirt again, cleaning herself off and cuddling against him once more. She was grateful that he'd done what he must to protect her from getting pregnant, but a tiny part of her wished that he hadn't. She loved Oliver more than anything, but she couldn't imagine what it would be like to give birth to the child of a man who wanted her, who wanted to be in the baby's life. She knew instinctively that Sebastian would be a wonderful father.

He wrapped his arms around her and pressed a sweet kiss on her head. "Thank you," he whispered.

She laughed hoarsely, realizing her throat was rough from crying out. "I feel like I'm the one who should be thanking you. Now I finally see what all the fuss was about."

He gave a huff of laughter. "I'm glad you liked it."

Snuggling closer, she laid her head on his chest, loving the way his heart thudded beneath her cheek. Overwhelmed with emotions, she simply let him hold her, the fireplace crackling beside them, still providing enough warmth that she wasn't ready to reach for a blanket just yet.

Words of tenderness... perhaps even love?... welled up in her throat. Whatever it was, she'd certainly never felt it before. But she tamped the emotions back because they were so very raw and new she didn't even know how to give voice to them.

*I have a lover*, she thought once more, and then she drifted off to sleep.

# Chapter Nineteen

Long after Jocelyn had fallen asleep, Sebastian lay staring up at the ceiling, letting his hand idly drift up and down her back. This evening had been everything he'd imagined it could be... right up until she'd said those things about marriage, about no one ever having to know they'd been together.

He didn't know why it had upset him so much. It wasn't as though he *wanted* to marry her.

Did he?

He supposed he just chafed at the reminder that he was holding a bloody countess in his arms. That he could never, not in a million years or after a dozen promotions, give her the kind of life that she already had without him. She didn't need him for anything other than his body.

That shouldn't bother him. Hell, he should be deliriously happy that she'd allowed him inside her, that she hadn't demanded anything of him in return.

Instead, he found himself wishing that this didn't have to end, that he could hold her in his arms every night.

What the hell was happening to him? What kind of a spell had she placed on him?

Or had he just finally fallen victim to the curse that had plagued humanity for millennia—love?

A shiver went through him at the thought, because if that was true, he'd fallen in an even tougher category—unrequited love.

With a groan, he carefully extricated himself from his sleeping countess and remade his bed, feeling odd to be doing it naked. Then he carried her there, placed her upon it, and climbed in next to her. She awoke for only a moment before smiling and snuggling against him once again.

Unable to stop from smiling himself, he hugged her close, pressed his face against her sweet-smelling hair, and fell asleep with her in his arms.

SEBASTIAN WOKE AS DAWN was breaking through the curtains of his bedroom. Jocelyn still lay beside him, her limbs intertwined with his. A strand of her hair tickled his nose, and he blew it away with a smile. He'd half-expected to wake and find last night was just a vivid, wonderful dream, but she was still here.

A soft sigh escaped her as she snuggled closer, like a kitten seeking warmth. His smile grew as he propped himself up on one arm and looked down at her, her wild auburn hair so vibrant against his white pillows, her lovely face so sweet and innocent in sleep.

*There is a countess in my bed.*

He still couldn't believe it, never would have been able to even imagine such a thing could be possible. He'd had so few good things in his life that having her here seemed too much.

Winding a strand of her silky hair around his fingertip, he brought it to his nose and breathed in deeply, loving her scent, vanilla and lavender. She smelled of peace and home, everything sweet and lovely that had been missing from his life for so long.

He'd had a few lovers in his day, and he'd spent a few nights with Marina before he'd been shipped off, but none of them had come even close to the sensual delights he'd shared with Jocelyn.

He'd tried to make himself be content with the idea that she'd come into his life just to show him he was capable of caring for someone again. That he would be free now to find another, more suitable woman to become his wife and bear his children, but he knew that she had ruined him for anyone else.

Jocelyn Layton was the woman he wanted, and he could never truly have her.

Oh, he could occasionally have her like this, a sweet tumble in his bed, but she'd as much as told him that she would never marry him, never let anyone know about their relationship. She would never be the mother of his children, a thought he found surprisingly painful, given he hadn't even thought of having children until recently.

She stretched and then blinked up at him, her green eyes owlish in her lovely face. "Good morning, Sebastian," she whispered, her face flaming as she no doubt realized that she was naked in his arms.

"Good morning, darling," he replied, kissing her playfully on the nose.

She grinned and scooted a bit away, tucking the sheet primly around her chest. "Did you carry me in here?"

He nodded. "I liked waking up with you by my side."

"I like it, too," she admitted. She shifted even further away from him, a troubled look crossing her face. "This is terribly embarrassing, but I really have to use the necessary."

"It's two doors down the hall. On the left," he informed her, relieved that her frown wasn't because she was regretting the entire encounter. "Would you like to borrow my robe?"

Her eyes widened almost comically. "It's not in the flat? You share it with other people?"

The differences in their lifestyles came crashing down upon him once again. Of course, she would find that odd. She'd probably never had to share a water closet in her life. How shocked she would be to find that most people in this neighborhood didn't have indoor plumbing at all, let alone the magnificent private chamber he'd caught a glimpse of when he was in her bedroom.

Truth be told, he'd been able to afford better than this place even before his promotion, but the better pay was still relatively new, and he was comfortable here. He'd lived in much worse places.

"I'll come with you and stand outside the door," he assured her quickly, suddenly thinking of her out in the hallway at the mercy of the rough denizens of his building. "I know it isn't what you're used to, but it will be fine."

She didn't look as though she believed him, but matters seemed to have reached a critical state because she allowed him to wrap her in his robe and lead her out of his flat and down the hall. Her face was a deep shade of scarlet as she closed the door behind her, and he felt a pang of embarrassment that he had nothing better to offer her.

Women like her were brought up to pretend like they didn't even have bodily functions. This must be humiliating for her.

Several minutes passed before she finally came out again. "Well, that was... unpleasant," she said shakily, and as he thought of how disgusting his fellow tenants could sometimes leave it, he could only imagine the worst.

"I'm sorry," he said, hurrying her back to his flat. "Next time, I'll go in first. Make sure it's clean for you."

Assuming there *was* a next time.

"It's fine," she said, her face still hot with embarrassment as he shut his door behind them. "Really. I just wasn't expecting... that."

He scrubbed his hand across his face and tried to think of how he could salvage the situation. "Can I make you some tea? Perhaps some eggs?"

"That would be lovely," she said, obviously grateful for the change of subject. "I'll just go get dressed."

She hurried over to where she'd left her bag, picked the clothes she'd hurriedly discarded last night off the floor, then hurried into his bedroom.

As soon as the bedroom door clicked behind her, he made his way into the little kitchen, lighting a fire in the stove and filling a kettle with the pitcher of water that he had to go to the communal water closet to fill. With a sigh, he put it on to boil, then ran down to use the water closet himself, shaking his head when he saw it was just as bad as he'd feared.

By the time he returned to his flat and scrambled up some eggs, his lovely little house guest had come out, looking somehow as neat and tidy as she had when she'd arrived last night.

He quickly put the eggs on two plates, then went over and

pulled her into a fierce hug. "I know this is uncomfortable for you. It is for me as well. But you look lovely, and I'm so very glad you came to see me last night."

"I'm glad, too," she said against his chest. "I'm certain I'll get used to the rest of this. Everything just seems so... intimate."

"Being lovers is a very intimate thing," he said, with a bit of a smile. But his smile faded as he thought of the other women he'd been with. With the others, there had been no slow, sensual lovemaking in front of the fire, no sleeping in each other's arms and waking up together. No, it had been a quick perfunctory coupling, followed by both parties going their separate ways.

*This is better. This is what I want. How could I ever have been satisfied with so much less?*

"Come, let's have some breakfast," he said, letting her go and returning to the stove to grab the plates of eggs, which he placed on his small table.

She sat primly across from him, so very much the countess. She'd probably never eaten eggs off an earthenware plate without the correct silverware setting and cloth napkins. He didn't even have napkins, and his silverware was mismatched and tarnished.

But she dug in heartily, not giving any indication that she'd expected more, and his heart gave a surge of something he hesitated to name.

She suddenly put her fork down and met his gaze. "I just realized that I went all evening without even once thinking of Evelyn." A rush of tears filled her eyes, and she dashed at them with the back of her hand. "I'm so grateful to you for providing me this escape from all those terrible thoughts and the grief, but I also feel guilty."

He put his own fork down and reached across the table to cover her hand with his. "Don't ever feel guilty for taking a break from the grief. I am certain that Evelyn would never begrudge you a night of passion."

"Perhaps not," she said shakily. "On some level, I know that. But it's still hard to even think about moving on without her."

"Try not to think of it like that," he said, and he felt a new rush of anger at The Viper for having caused so much sorrow. "Think of it as simply surviving."

She nodded and picked her fork back up, taking a few more bites before offering him a hesitant smile. "These eggs are quite good. Thank you."

"You're welcome."

THEY ATE IN SILENCE for a while, but then Jocelyn pushed her empty plate away and met Sebastian's gaze. She'd felt entirely out of her element since the moment she'd awakened. "I don't really the know the etiquette in situations like this. What do we talk about the morning after a night like last night?"

He gave her a burning look. "I wouldn't know. I've never had a night like last night. And I've never had a woman stay the night with me. Other than my wife, of course."

"Of course," she murmured, blushing hotly. She was glad that last night had been special for him as well. "When would you like to do this again?"

"As soon as possible," he said, reaching across the table

to squeeze her hand. "But first, I need to find better accommodations. I can't ask you to come here again. I realize now how difficult it must have been for you."

"It wasn't difficult at all," she hastened to assure him, though she shuddered internally at the thought of the horrible communal bathroom. However, that seemed a small price to pay for the wonderful night of lovemaking and companionship.

He grimaced. "I know that you probably never wanted something like this, not with someone like me. You're the kind of woman who was made to be a wife and mother. I want you to know that if... the measures I took to protect you tonight didn't work... if you found yourself with child, I would do the right thing. I would marry you."

She frowned and drew her hand away, her heart pounding frantically at the very thought. "I didn't like being a wife. In fact, I hated being a wife."

He sank back in his chair, his face going completely blank, something she'd realized he did when he was feeling too much. "So, you'd rather face complete disgrace and have a child out of wedlock than wed someone like me," he said evenly, the lack of inflection alerting her to how much she'd hurt him.

She thought of the night they'd just spent together, the absolute delight she felt in his arms, the comfort and safety he emanated. "That's not what I'm saying," she tried to tell him. "I'm just saying that not many women get to be in the position I'm in, living comfortably and not having to answer to any man. I wouldn't want to give that up if it wasn't an absolute necessity."

But being pregnant would make it one. Despite all her

newfound courage, she'd never be brave enough to face the social backlash of being pregnant and unwed.

"I understand," he said stiffly, though she could see that he didn't. Not at all. He thought that she didn't want to marry him, in particular, either because of his background or his small flat and public water closet. He had no idea how hard it was to be a woman and have no power or money of your own.

And then and there, she decided she would get involved in Evelyn's cause. A woman should never have to choose between love and independence.

*Love.*

The thought brought her up short, and as she gazed across the table at this man she'd known for such a short time, she realized she'd fallen head over heels for him. He'd turned all her thoughts about love upside down, and she didn't want to go back to living her life without him.

"Sebastian," she said softly, ready to take it all back, ready perhaps even to tell him how much she cared, but he pushed suddenly to his feet, his chair making a terrible screech.

"It's nearly nine," he said stiffly. "I'll walk you out."

# Chapter Twenty

J ocelyn sank back against the seat of her carriage, watching as Sebastian's building narrowed to a mere dot in the distance, overwhelmed by all the thoughts and emotions racing through her head. Her carriage had arrived promptly at nine, as she'd asked, but it had taken every bit of her strength to leave Sebastian's side, despite their rather squalid surroundings and the way they'd parted.

Last night had been the single most eye-opening, exciting event of her life.

All she wanted to do was repeat it as often as she could.

In his arms, she didn't feel like the good girl she'd always worked to be, the stickler for rules and etiquette. She didn't feel like she had to please everyone else. She need only please herself and her lover, and the entire world could go hang.

Being with him was selfish and perhaps even foolish, but for the first time in her life, she didn't care. He made her happy when her life had become such a dark and sorrowful place. She couldn't regret a moment she spent with him.

She hated that she'd hurt his feelings in the end, and she knew she had to find a way to make him understand that her aversion to marriage had nothing to do with him. If she were ever going to shackle herself to a man again, it would be him.

But why should she have to? As long as they were careful, she could continue to see him. She liked the way things were. She didn't know why he'd gotten so upset. Men weren't supposed to truly want to be married, were they?

For a few minutes longer, she let her mind drift back to the bliss she'd found with him, dreaming of when they could do it again. But finally, she forced herself to think about all the other things she'd abandoned last night.

She had a son to see to. And she had to check on Abbie.

The realities of her world came crashing back down upon her before his flat was even completely out of sight. She was not some worldly courtesan who could sleep all day in her lover's arms. She was a mother, a countess. A thousand duties and responsibilities were waiting for her.

With a sigh, she pulled the lap blanket tighter around her, shivering in the February cold now that Sebastian was not here to warm her.

She still couldn't believe she'd gone so many hours without thinking of Evelyn. Guilt welled up within her once again, despite Sebastian's words, but on the heels of the guilt came a surge of fury as well.

She had no doubt that Sebastian, Drake, and Quinn were doing their best to catch the bastard who had murdered her sister, but if Sebastian's suspicions were right, if The Viper was Viscount Danbury, his hands were tied. All of theirs were.

Mortimer was not only Drake's brother, but he was a viscount, a member of Parliament. He probably wouldn't even consent to speak to Sebastian, and without a confession, there really wasn't enough evidence against him to make an arrest.

*He would talk to me.*

The thought took hold and circled wildly around and around in her brain. He'd been overly solicitous of her at the funeral, insisting she call upon him if she needed anything. She had no doubt if she went to his home, he'd agree to see her.

What would he tell her if she asked the right questions? Could she get him to admit that he'd had something to do with Evelyn's death? Could she at least get him to admit that Evelyn had turned down his proposal all those years ago?

If he really was The Viper, it would be very dangerous. But she'd take Thomas and her driver, Jarvis, with her. He couldn't very well kill her with her servants waiting outside. In fact, she'd tell them to insist upon seeing her if she wasn't out in thirty minutes.

The idea of actually doing something, of making some progress on her own toward finding out who had done this to her sister, filled her with a sense of purpose that she'd been badly lacking since all this had happened.

A part of her wanted to have her coachman head there right now, but she was desperately in need of a bath and a change of clothes. And even she knew she wasn't thinking clearly right now. No, she needed to go home, clean up, and perhaps take a nap. Then she'd very carefully plot out what she planned to say to Mortimer Blackstone when she saw him.

SEBASTIAN WAS LATE to the office that morning, which was quite unlike him, but he didn't care. He'd been working long hours every day since he'd gotten this job. Seeing Jocelyn off after their night together was the least he could do. She'd obviously had not idea of the sort of hours he kept when she'd told her footman to come back for her at nine. Usually, he'd have been at work for hours by then. But how could she know, when she'd come from generations of people who'd never had to work a day in their lives? There was no way he was going to leave her alone in his flat with the sort of riff-raff who resided in his building, so he'd had to stay until she left. And then he'd had to spend an appreciable amount of time talking himself out of being hurt and furious that she didn't want to marry him.

He'd known from the beginning what this was, so he had no idea why her words this morning had upset him so. He was so far beneath her socially that they should not have even met, let alone done all the sinful, beautiful things they'd done last night. He'd be a fool to let his stung pride keep him from arranging to meet with her again just as soon as possible.

As he settled behind his desk and stared blankly at the piles of paperwork in front of him, he thought about the realization he'd come to after the water closet incident. If he was going to continue his relationship with the beautiful widow, he was going to have to buy a house of his own. He wouldn't ask her to keep coming to see him in his seedy little flat, to use the filthy communal water closet down the hall.

Of course, anything he could afford would be nothing like she was used to, but he did have a nice little nest egg saved up, and he could definitely entertain her somewhere far nicer than he had last night.

"Pond," he bellowed.

Constable Pond came rushing in moments later, his face pale. "Sir?" he asked with a squeak.

"I need to talk to an estate agent. Would you arrange that for me?"

Obviously having expected something far more alarming, Pond swallowed visibly. "Yes, sir. Of course." He turned to leave, then paused. "Inspector O'Brien phoned for you."

Sebastian frowned and looked up. "What did he say?"

"He said he wants to speak with you as soon as possible. He said it had something to do with the lock."

Excitement surged through Sebastian, and he stood and put the coat he'd just taken off back on. "Excellent news, Pond! We might just catch that bastard yet!"

Pond nodded, flushing as he backed out the door. "Of course, sir! I never doubted it."

HALF AN HOUR LATER, Sebastian was seated in O'Brien's study, making polite chit-chat with his friend and Allison while inwardly chafing at the bit for O'Brien to dispense with the pleasantries and get to the damned point. He hadn't rushed over here to talk about their charity work, though he was glad that O'Brien was finding things to occupy his time since his injury.

"Should we tell him?" Allison asked, drawing Sebastian's attention as she turned her shining gaze on her husband, nearly vibrating with excitement.

"Tell me what?" Sebastian asked cautiously, a little taken aback by Allison's intensity.

O'Brien cleared his throat, his own eyes suspiciously bright. "We've just found out that we'll be parents come summertime."

Relief washed through Sebastian. He didn't know what he'd expected, but this truly was wonderful news. Though once again, he felt a bit of a pang at the thought that his own hopes of starting a family were getting further and further away. Especially if he continued his affair with Jocelyn. After their conversation this morning, he'd have to be more careful than ever that their time spent together did not result in a child. She'd made her opinion on the matter quite clear.

Jocelyn did not want his child.

He blinked the thoughts away and smiled at his friends. "That's wonderful news! Thank you for telling me."

Allison grinned and stood, then leaned down and gave her husband a kiss on the forehead. "Well, I'll leave you two to discuss whatever's got Sebastian all in a froth. I just wanted to tell you our good news."

O'Brien watched her leave, his once-taciturn face now glowing with happiness.

"She's good for you," Sebastian observed.

"I'm a lucky man," O'Brien agreed. Then he became all business as he opened the top drawer of his desk and pulled out a lock that looked identical to the broken one they'd found at the murder scene. "I had some free time yesterday, so I went looking for places that sold this sort of lock. Luckily for us, I could only find one."

Sebastian picked up the lock and turned it around and around in his hand. "Did the proprietor remember who'd bought one recently?"

O'Brien's face fell a bit. "Unfortunately, although he said he'd only sold one in the past few weeks, he didn't have a clear memory of who bought it, other than that it was a toff with dark hair. Of course, that description could fit any number of people, but when I described Viscount Danbury to him, he agreed that it sounded like the right man."

Deflated, Sebastian sank back in his chair. "Well, I don't suppose it's reasonable to expect that the shopkeeper would remember every person who's come in to their establishment in the last few weeks, nor require their name before they purchase something."

"It's him," O'Brien said, his features hardening. "That bastard murdered those girls, caused my accident, and now, he's bloody laughing at us."

"I think so, too," Sebastian agreed. "But we have no proof."

O'Brien sighed, turning in his chair to look at all the photographs and scribblings pinned on the wall behind him. "There has to be something we're missing. Something that will prove that he's The Viper."

Sebastian stood and walked closer himself, shaking his head. "There's nothing, is there? He's going to just keep killing these girls, and there is nothing we can do about it."

"You could put a man on him, have him watched constantly. If he really is The Viper, he'll try and strike again, and then maybe we can catch him in the act."

"I could put Pond on it," Sebastian said, nodding. "He's so nondescript no one would ever notice him lurking around."

"That's a good idea," O'Brien agreed. "It's time you gave the lad a little more to do than fetch coffee and answer the phone."

"Perhaps you're right." Sebastian drew his gaze away from the wall and met his friend's gaze. "Do you think there's any chance he'll go after Joc—" He cleared his throat. "Lady Aston?"

O'Brien smiled grimly. "You're on a first-name basis with the countess now?"

Sebastian thought about denying it, but what was the point? O'Brien was far too astute to lie to about something like that.

"We've grown... close," Sebastian admitted, afraid he was blushing as much as fair-skinned Jocelyn always did. "I've been trying to offer her comfort for her sister's death. I want to solve this thing for her. But I'm worried that she could be in danger, too."

O'Brien sighed. "Well, I'm the last person who could chide you for reaching too high. But I don't think Lady Aston is in danger. I don't think she's ever rejected the man."

"I'm not aiming too high," Sebastian hastened to reassure him. "I have no expectations. I know a woman like her is entirely out of my reach." All of that was true, which only made his behavior this morning even more ridiculous.

Shaking his head, O'Brien laughed. "Oh, my friend, you've got it bad."

In response, Sebastian could only nod glumly. "Yes, I suppose I do."

They sat in silence for a few moments, and then Sebastian shook his head. "Bloody hell. I I need to talk to Blackstone, don't I? See what he knows, if anything. Perhaps he really doesn't have any idea that it could be his brother."

"He's been acting like he knows," O'Brien said. "I think you'd be making a big mistake to go to him. Either way, it's likely to end with you losing your job."

"Perhaps," Sebastian agreed. "But I don't see any other way. I will never be able to do this on my own. It has to come from the top for a man like Danbury. Even if he is Blackstone's brother."

O'Brien nodded pensively. "I'd like to believe that Drake is a good man. We've been friends for a lot of years. But when loyalties are tested, you never know which will win out."

"I guess I'm just going to have to take my chances," Sebastian said grimly. "I still have one more avenue to explore, but either way, I'll go speak with him tomorrow. Wish me luck."

SEBASTIAN LEFT O'BRIEN'S house more convinced than ever that The Viper was Viscount Danbury. He made a quick stop by his flat to pick up Evelyn's diary, taking it back to the office, where he pored over it for hours, reading back through Evelyn's life until he found an entry she'd written when she was eighteen.

*M, the V of D, cornered me at the E of K's ball last night. He asked me to walk outside with him, and although I had no desire to do so, he seemed quite desperate to talk to me. Once he got me in a remote corner of the garden, he tried to kiss me. When I pushed him away, he grew quite furious, told me he'd always planned to make me his wife. When I told him that I did not want to be anyone's wife, he became so angry and cold he frightened me. I am more convinced than ever that I did the right thing.*

He cursed Evelyn's penchant for using initials instead of spelling out names. He couldn't prove that she was speaking about Danbury, but how many other men whose first names started with M were also the viscount of someplace that started with a D?

Of course, this wasn't the sort of proof that would stand up in court, but surely this was enough to convince Blackstone, who obviously already had his suspicions.

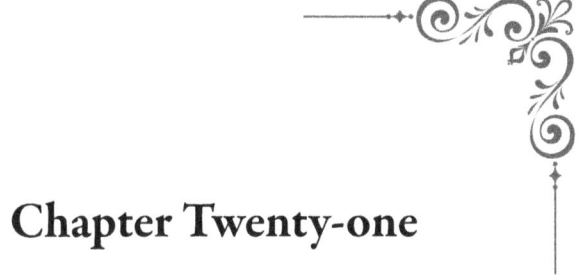

# Chapter Twenty-one

After having thought about it all evening, her certainty about his guilt growing with each remembered exchange, Jocelyn decided to pay Mortimer Blackstone a visit the next afternoon.

Even though his townhouse was easily within walking distance of her own, she decided to take her carriage, along with Jarvis and Thomas, as planned, just so that she would not be completely alone with the old family friend who she was now certain had been the one to murder her sister.

"Jarvis, Thomas, remember," she instructed the coachman and the footman as she got out of the carriage in front of the Blackstone house, "if I haven't come back out within thirty minutes, I need you to come in after me."

Jarvis and Thomas exchanged looks, then nodded grimly.

"My lady, it seems as if you're putting yourself in a dangerous situation," Jarvis dared to say.

Thomas chimed in as well, "My lady, are you certain you shouldn't leave this to the inspector?"

She squared her shoulders, though inside, she was somewhat worried about that herself. "I'm just going to talk to the man. I'm sure I'll be fine."

Even though it seemed more and more likely that

Mortimer was The Viper, she still couldn't really imagine the foppish dandy she'd known all her life actually being able to hurt anyone. Maybe she was wrong about him. She wanted to be wrong.

Far easier to believe it had been a faceless stranger who'd performed these atrocities, not someone she'd played with as a child. If Mortimer really was the villain she thought, how could she ever trust anyone ever again?

Leaving her worried servants with the coach, she strode to the front steps and knocked loudly on the door. This was highly improper, to just show up without an invitation outside of calling hours, let alone a socially acceptable reason for showing up unannounced, but she wanted to throw him off guard from the start.

As she waited, she realized how far she'd come from worrying about the lack of place cards at Allison's wedding just a few short weeks ago.

So much had changed in her life, and now, she couldn't imagine ever going back.

After a moment, the huge door creaked open, and Mortimer's butler blinked down at her. "Yes, my lady? May I help you?"

"I'm the Countess of Aston. I'm here to see Viscount Danbury."

The butler frowned. "I'll see if he's at home."

In order to keep her mind off the dangers of what she was doing, Jocelyn focused on the ridiculousness of that statement and wondered why it was so socially acceptable. They both knew Mortimer was home. What the butler was really checking was whether he'd consent to see her.

He left her waiting in the foyer like an unwelcome, unexpected visitor, which she supposed she was, though she was not used to such treatment. After what seemed an interminable time, the butler finally returned. "Right this way, my lady."

She followed him to a parlor done in shades of gold. The room was lovely, but had the scent and feel of not having been used for quite some time. Probably since their mother had died. What use did two bachelors have for a room like this, which was meant for the lady of the house to receive callers?

Sitting gingerly on the edge of the divan, her heart thundering in her chest, Jocelyn waited for Mortimer to put in an appearance. Her attention caught on her reflection in a mirror across the room, and she wondered idly whether anyone could tell by looking at her that she'd taken a lover.

*My lover.*

She didn't know why she'd become so enamored of those words, but she had. She loved to think them, and she loved to say them.

Perhaps she'd become enamored of more than just the words.

Before she could explore that thought any further, Mortimer opened the door and strode in, sending a icy rush through her veins.

"Jocelyn," he said with a smile. "To what do I owe the pleasure?"

She swallowed dryly. "You said if I needed anything...."

He nodded and crossed the room to her side, sitting down on the divan beside her, the dainty piece of furniture creaking under their combined weight. "Of course, my dear. What can I do to help?"

She gazed into his dark eyes and shivered at the complete lack of emotion. His features were composed into an expression of concern, but she did not see that reflected in his eyes. It chilled her to the bone.

"I just needed to talk to you about Evelyn." She didn't have to fake the way her voice broke on her sister's name. She still couldn't say it without tearing up.

"Of course, my dear," he murmured, patting her hand. "I'm glad you felt you could come to me."

She steeled herself not to pull away, even though his touch made her skin crawl. Was she sitting with pure evil? Could this man really have done those horrific things to Evelyn and the others? Looking into those eyes, she could believe it.

"I just can't believe that such a thing happened," she said, her voice shaking. "Who would want to hurt sweet Evelyn? She never harmed anyone. She was so kind, and she spent all her time trying to make the world a better place."

He made a noncommittal sound, still patting her hand.

"I just don't understand how someone could be so depraved, so completely soulless to do such a thing."

*There.* She finally saw a flicker of something in those sharklike eyes. A flare of... pride?

"I think it's rather amazing that he's been doing this for months, yet is no closer to being caught than he was in the beginning," he said, and his tacit approval of the monster made her even more convinced that he *was* the monster.

"Oh, I don't know about that," she couldn't help but jab. "I think that the police might have a few ideas about who he might be."

His eyes sharpened. "Well, I certainly hope they catch him then."

*Do you?*

She dropped her gaze and fiddled with the tips of her gloves, wondering what else she could say to try and force him to make some sort of confession. She was treading a dangerous line, and while she didn't want to fall off the edge, she also didn't want to leave here without something she could use to make sure this bastard didn't hurt anyone else.

"You must be feeling sad as well, aren't you?" she finally asked. "Since you and Evelyn were all but promised to each other as children?"

He finally took his hand off hers. "Pardon me?"

"I always thought you and Evelyn had been promised to each other. Was that not the case?" she asked, forging on, despite the sudden ice in his tone.

"Certainly not. If so, it would have happened years ago, don't you think?" He smiled but there was no warmth behind it. "I think we both know that your sister was not suited to be the wife of a viscount."

The utter disdain with which he said the last infuriated her, even if it was partly true, but she fought to keep her anger at bay. She couldn't let him know that this was anything other than what it appeared—two old friends discussing a tragic loss.

"Perhaps. It's just that before she died, Evelyn told her friend she was going to meet the man whose proposal she'd turned down. I didn't know who that could be. She never mentioned that anyone had proposed to her."

He pushed to his feet and strode across the room, looking out the window at the garden below. "Is that why you truly came here today? To accuse me of being the man she met with?" His voice still sounded calm, but she could tell that she'd rattled him a bit.

"No, of course not. I told you, I came here because I just needed someone to talk to and you said that if I needed anything..." She trailed off, suddenly worried that she'd played the wrong card. Until now, he hadn't known that they had any reason to suspect him.

"Evelyn must have made someone very angry," he said, turning to look at her, his eyes narrowed. "I heard what happened to her. How she was brutalized. I don't think someone would do that if they hadn't harbored a grudge against her for a very long time."

She swallowed. Was that a confession? Could she get him to say more?

"Whoever she met with must have had a very fragile ego," she pressed on. "What sort of man would be so upset about something that must have happened half a dozen years ago? If she thought him unworthy of her then, I'm certain she felt the same now. She must have told him to quit bothering her, that she had no intention of becoming his wife, and he killed her for it."

"Evelyn never did know when to guard her tongue," he snapped, his careful façade cracking and letting her see what lay beneath his foppish exterior. It terrified her. She never should have come here alone, and she wondered if that had been Evelyn's last thought as well.

———— ⟊ ————

SEBASTIAN HAD THOUGHT about his evidence, or lack

of it, all night, but the next day, after doing a few pressing things that couldn't wait, he'd hailed a hackney and instructed the driver to head toward Scotland Yard. His mind whirled with what he'd say to Blackstone when he got there.

How did one accuse a man's brother of such horrific crimes? Especially since he had so little proof to offer.

Danbury's first name started with M. He was a member of The Viper Club. He'd possibly proposed to Evelyn Lindsay, though no one knew for certain. And someone matching his description had bought the lock that had been on the gardener's shed. The only real damning evidence he had was the diary entry, and that only made sense if Blackstone believed Evelyn had been referring to his brother.

The more he thought about it, the more ridiculous it seemed to accuse a viscount of being a horrific killer on such flimsy circumstantial evidence.

Still, his gut was screaming at him that he was right. And how could he ever live with himself if yet another girl was murdered when he could have done something to stop it?

By the time he got to Scotland Yard, he'd almost talked himself out of it, only to find that Blackstone hadn't shown up that day, saying he was going to be working on something at home.

The irregularity of that spiked his suspicions once more. Blackstone never missed work, and the fact that he'd done so now only solidified Sebastian's theory that Blackstone suspected Danbury, too, and was trying to stop him.

He had to believe Blackstone wanted to stop the bastard.

If his boss was merely trying to cover up his brother's crimes, Sebastian knew he could kiss his job goodbye.

Deciding he'd cross that bridge when he came to it and for once give someone the benefit of the doubt, he left Scotland Yard in another hack and headed to Mayfair, where Blackstone shared a townhouse with his brother.

Sebastian would have to tread carefully. He had no idea whether Danbury would be there or not, and he certainly couldn't talk to Blackstone about this if he was. Instead, he'd just update his boss on what he'd learned about the key as his reason for showing up at his home even though that wasn't at all proper procedure.

He was still mulling through it all when he arrived at Blackstone's imposing brick townhouse, and it didn't escape him that it was just one block away from Postman's Park. However, everything he'd been thinking came to a crashing halt when he recognized Jocelyn's carriage sitting out front.

Blood rushed in his ears as he leaped out of the hack, paying the driver without conscious thought, his entire focus on the fact that Evelyn was here, with the Blackstones, one of which he was almost certain was a murderer. Moreover, her coachman and footman were gesturing at him to approach. Oh, this was bad, very bad.

What the hell was she doing here?

Striding over to the carriage, he met the footman's nervous gaze. "Thomas, is it?" he asked.

"Yes, Inspector, but how do you know my name?" The strapping young man looked completely flabbergasted.

"It's my business to know such things," Sebastian said impatiently. "Now, what in the devil is the countess doing here?"

The man didn't pretend not to know what he was talking

about, but the coachman, Jarvis, added his voice. "We don't know, Inspector, but she said that if she hadn't come out in half an hour, we was to go in after her. Sir, we have no weapons or authority in a nobleman's house, so it seems most providential that you have come."

So she knew it was dangerous. She knew, and she went in anyway.

He'd severely underestimated her desire to see her sister's killer brought to justice.

"How long has it been?" he asked, already striding toward the front door.

"Twenty-five minutes, sir," the footman called after him. "We were getting nervous."

"I should say so." Sebastian attacked the brass door knocker and, for good effect, rang the bell as well. When the butler opened the door, Sebastian flashed his warrant card in the man's face and strode past him before he could say a word to deny him. He threw open several doors that led off the hall, finding them empty, until the fourth one brought him into a sitting room that held Danbury and Jocelyn. The relief in her eyes when she saw him told him everything he needed to know. Behind him, he heard the butler bellowing for help.

"What are you doing here, Ness?" Danbury demanded, his dark eyes snapping with fury.

Sebastian ignored him and strode directly to Jocelyn, pulling her to her feet and stepping protectively in front of her. He was both angry at her for coming here and grateful that she was all right. If anything had happened to her... He hated to think of what he'd do.

"I asked you a question!" Danbury strode toward him, and

Sebastian saw that the evil inside him was very close to the surface. Whatever Jocelyn had said to him, it had hit a nerve.

"I don't answer to you," Sebastian fired back.

Danbury laughed, a deep, braying sound with a hint of madness. "Well, you do answer to my brother, and he is not going to appreciate that you forced your way inside our home."

"I'm protecting Lady Aston." Sebastian pushed open his coat, revealing his revolver. "So I suggest you get out of our way."

"What are you protecting her from?" Danbury demanded, that wild light growing in his eyes.

"I think you know," Sebastian said coldly, his patience wearing thin. Violence seethed right below the surface. All the months of trying to figure out The Viper's identity, and now here he stood, and there wasn't a damn thing he could do about it. He almost wished the bastard would attack him.

"Do you think you're here to arrest me?" Danbury raised a brow, his voice dripping with disdain. "I'll have your job for your insolence."

The bastard was only a few feet away, so close Sebastian could see the sweat breaking out on his high forehead.

"I don't give a damn about my job," Sebastian snarled. "I should kill you now for what you've done."

"If you touch a hair on my head, it will be you on the gallows, not me," Danbury smirked.

Sebastian's fist struck the smug bastard's jaw before the thought had even truly taken root in his mind. Danbury stumbled backward, a murderous look in his eyes, but before either man could do more, Blackstone's voice rang furiously through the room.

"What is the meaning of this!" Blackstone stood in the doorway, flanked by two burly footmen, his expression wintry. "Ness! Explain yourself."

"He barged in here with the most ridiculous accusations," Danbury claimed, pressing a hand to his face, suddenly looking once again like the mild-mannered viscount.

Sebastian's heart sank as he realized how this looked. How could he have let his anger get the best of him? He'd punched Blackstone's brother in his own home. He'd be lucky if he didn't go to jail for this. He turned to Jocelyn, saddened to see that she looked even more frightened than when he'd arrived. Had his violence disgusted her?

"You need to go home immediately... to your child," he said firmly, determined to get her out of here before he answered for his actions. "Your nanny rang the station looking for you. Your son has a... rash. Something he ate perhaps?"

She played along, nodding jerkily, obviously glad to be able to escape the seething undercurrent of danger in the room. "Yes, I must go." With one last lingering look at Sebastian, she turned and fled the room.

"Only a coward kills unarmed women," Sebastian muttered darkly to Danbury the moment Jocelyn shut the front door behind her. "I won't rest until you pay for what you've done."

"Drake, rein in your man," Danbury demanded, looking across the room to where his brother still stood in the doorway, his expression completely blank.

Sebastian had absolutely no idea what Blackstone would say next. Would he protect his brother, or did his loyalty still lay on the side of the law?

"Go on about your day," Blackstone told Danbury at last. "I

know that his actions have been inexcusable, but rest assured, I will handle my man."

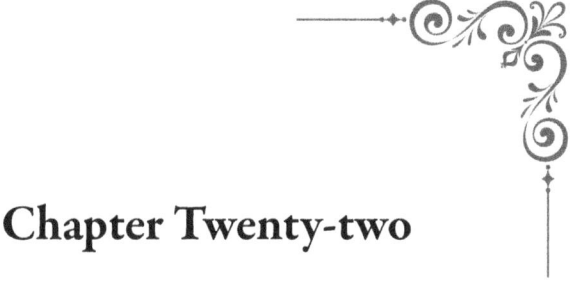

# Chapter Twenty-two

Blackstone led Sebastian grimly down a hallway and then into a dark wood-paneled study. Wordlessly, he shut the door, then took the chair behind his desk, motioning for Sebastian to have the seat across from him.

Sebastian remained standing, still trembling with rage. He had no intention of "being handled."

"You know why I'm here," Sebastian said, keeping his voice pitched low in case Danbury was outside the door. "You know what he's done."

"You're a fool," Blackstone said, his features inscrutable. "What do you think you've gained by coming here? By punching a viscount in the face?"

"How long have you known?" Sebastian demanded.

"That's just it," Blackstone said, his façade crumbling a bit. "I don't know anything. I just have a feeling. Do you think want to believe this of my own brother? I've been trying to prove it wrong."

"I've been trying to prove it right," Sebastian replied. "I'm not having any luck either."

Blackstone scrubbed a hand over his face. "What do you have on him? I assume there's something, or you wouldn't have had the gall to come here, to his home."

Reaching into the interior pocket of his tweed vest, Sebastian pulled out Evelyn's diary. Flipping through the pages, he found the one he'd earmarked and put it on Blackstone's desk. "Read this."

Blackstone leaned forward, his dark eyes scanning the page before he met Sebastian's stare, a look of relief passing across his face. "So? What does that prove?"

"Evelyn told her friend Heather Fields that she was going to meet the man who'd been harassing her, whose proposal she'd turned down, the day before she went missing." He flipped the diary to the last entry. "Then she wrote this on the very day she went missing."

Blackstone sank back in his seat, looking as though he'd had the wind punched out of him. "It still proves nothing, but I'm afraid you're right."

Frustration built within Sebastian. "Tell me what you know. You obviously suspect him. You did everything in your power to turn my investigation in any direction other than his."

"I was trying to protect you, not him," Blackstone claimed. "I can't go after someone like Danbury for this, even if he is my brother, without irrefutable proof. You know how the system works. You know that a judge would scoff if we tried to prosecute a peer with the evidence we have. Then he'd go free and spend the rest of his days trying to bring us down while still... doing what he's doing."

"Murdering young girls," Sebastian said sharply. "That's what he's doing."

"I know!" Drake said explosively. "I hoped I was wrong. Prayed I was. But I knew Polly Keys had been his mistress. I knew how angry he'd been when she'd broken things off with him. I first suspected when O'Brien showed me the snuff box. I've gone through his things and can't find his, and he used to have it with him all the time. But more than that, I just know him. He's always been... different. When we were children, he killed things. Cats. Squirrels. Our pet dog. A girl in the village near our country estate who'd rejected him was found murdered... in much the same way as the girls here."

"And you did nothing." Shaking his head in disgust, Sebastian stared at him intently. "So why should I trust you with this? Why shouldn't I go to the commissioner himself?"

"With what? A few coincidences and diary entries that don't even mention him by name? You know you'd get nowhere. Worse yet, he might demand that you be locked up or fired for hitting him." Blackstone poured them both a drink from the crystal decanter on his desk and pushed Sebastian's toward him with a hand that was less than steady. "I can't keep you from going to the commissioner, but I can promise you that I want to make the bastard pay for this even more than you do. I'm doing everything I can to see him brought to justice. I just need you to give me a little more time."

Sebastian took a drink of Blackstone's very fine Irish whisky, staring down the man as he tried to put himself in his shoes. Was Blackstone simply trying to protect his brother, or did he really want to stop him just as badly as Sebastian and O'Brien did?

"You have to start working with me and O'Brien, not against us," Sebastian said in resignation, finally taking his seat. Either way, Blackstone was right. They couldn't do this without him and his connections. The commissioner would not want to touch this case with a ten-foot pole if he tried to go over

Blackstone's head. Danbury was a bloody viscount. He was practically untouchable.

"I need you to know that until this afternoon, until I overheard your conversation and you showed me Evelyn's diary, I didn't know for certain. All I had were suspicions. I wasn't trying to get in the way of your investigation, I just wanted to be the one to question the countess."

Now Sebastian understood. "You want to be the arresting officer. You want to handle the details as delicately as possible when the newspapers get wind of this. You want to be known as the man who arrested his own brother, rather than the brother of a murderer who did not take action."

"Yes!" For once, Blackstone let his guard down and allowed Sebastian a glimpse of how much this had to have been eating him up inside. "More than all of that, Evelyn was a friend. It kills me that this happened to her."

"You're in extreme danger, sir, staying in his proximity."

"I'll risk it for the payoff. If my name is to be sensationalized in the papers, let it be as a man of action, not one who let his brother the killer slip past his investigation."

*His investigation? It's my investigation.*

Sebastian nodded. This was about more than just the murders; it was about politics, reputation, and fame. For a few moments, he saw the situation from Blackstone's side of the desk and understood that at the heart of everything, his boss didn't want his name to become as infamous as his brother's after the eventual arrest. He undoubtedly had political aspirations that went higher than the assistant police commissioner, and his brother's villainy could ruin everything he'd worked for.

They sat in silence for a long time, finishing off their drinks, as Sebastian's mind raced with everything that he'd learned today, along with his fear for the woman he now knew that he loved.

"Sir, I don't care who plays the hero here. I'll take the rear. I'll have your back in all this if that's what you want. But what are we going to do to make that bastard stop?" Sebastian asked at last. "I can't live with any more blood on my hands."

"Neither can I," Blackstone said grimly. "But I have a plan."

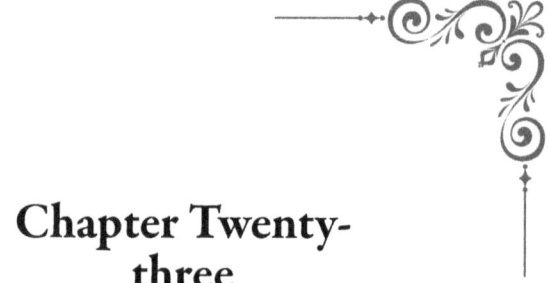

# Chapter Twenty-three

*He did it. Mortimer Blackstone killed my sister.*

Jocelyn sank back against the seat of her carriage as it jerked into motion, knowing that she'd just been face to face with a monster. Tremors started deep inside her and spread, until she was shivering from far more than the cold. Wrapping her arms around her, she blinked back the sting of tears, determined not to give into them.

She never should have gone to see Mortimer. She should have known that he'd never confess. All she'd done was make things worse, put herself in danger, and perhaps Sebastian as well.

*I'm sorry, Evelyn. I don't know what else to do.*

The tears came then despite her best efforts, and she cried deep, wrenching sobs as she thought of Evelyn going to meet with Mortimer, thinking him just an annoyance, having had no idea that she was meeting The Viper. How she must have suffered. How it must have pained her to know that someone she'd trusted could do something so terrible.

By the time she reached her house, just blocks away, her fear had ramped up to nearly an unbearable level. The moment she arrived, she summoned her butler Winston into her small office at the back of the house. "Winston, I have reason to believe that the monster who killed my sister might come after me next."

He mutely handed her a handkerchief, and she hastily blew her nose and scrubbed the tears from her face as best she could. "I want all the doors locked at all times," she continued, trembling. "I want one of the footmen on both the front and back doors, monitoring who comes in or out. Let no one but Inspector Ness and Allison and Quinn O'Brien in. I especially want you to make sure that neither of the Blackstone brothers are allowed to enter, no matter what they say."

Winston raised his eyebrows at that, but in true butler fashion, he didn't comment any further. "Of course, my lady. Anything else?"

"I think I'd like an additional footman in the hallway outside my room," she said, her heart still thundering in her ears at the danger she'd put herself in.

"Yes, my lady," he replied, turning toward the door. But then he paused and looked back at her. "Your entire staff loves you, my lady. We'll keep you safe."

"Thank you, Winston," she murmured, sinking into her chair. "Can you send Abbie and Oliver to me?"

She would keep those she loved as close to her as possible and hope that Winston was right.

SEBASTIAN AND BLACKSTONE had left Blackstone's townhouse, where it wasn't safe to talk, and gone to O'Brien's home in Belgravia. There the three men had talked about their plan to bring down Danbury for hours, until Sebastian finally felt that he could trust that Blackstone's plan might work. Far better than just going to the commissioner and hoping the man would do something about it with next to no evidence.

The sun had already set by the time they stood in O'Brien's entryway, waiting for Blackstone's carriage to be brought around.

"It's a good plan," Sebastian told Blackstone grudgingly. "But I'm still worried."

"As I am," Blackstone admitted tightly. "But I don't know what else to do."

"Nor do I." Before he could say more, he caught sight of Allison's lady's maid, Heather Fields, coming down the hall. "Miss Fields," he said, nodding to her. "Thank you for your help the other day."

Miss Fields changed direction, her lovely face troubled. "Were you able to find out who Evelyn met with?"

Sebastian exchanged glances with Blackstone. "We're working on it."

Heather's gaze went to Blackstone, and Sebastian felt compelled to make the introductions. "Mandrake Blackstone, the Assistant Metropolitan Police Commissioner. Blackstone, Miss Heather Fields."

"Pleasure to meet you, Miss Fields," Blackstone said politely, though Sebastian could tell he was wondering why he was being introduced to a lady's maid.

She managed a smile and a curtsy, though Sebastian could tell she was still upset about her friend. "Well, I hope you find out who did this before he strikes again," she said, then glanced over her shoulder. "I'd best be going, but it was nice to see you again, Inspector."

"Who was that?" Blackstone asked as she hurried away.

"Allison's lady's maid," Sebastian answered as he saw the carriage pull up outside through the leaded glass windows on either side of the door. "She was great friends with Evelyn. She's the one who told me what Evelyn said about meeting with the man whose proposal she'd turned down."

Blackstone stared after her for a moment, then nodded and went outside. "Would you rather I dropped you off at the precinct or your flat?"

"Take me to Lady Aston's," Sebastian replied, not caring what Blackstone thought of it. "I need to be certain she's safe."

Blackstone looked a little taken aback but didn't argue. To Sebastian's relief, the other man didn't say anything at all as the carriage made its way to Jocelyn's townhome. He imagined the man was haunted too much by his own thoughts at the moment to wonder about Sebastian's relationship with Jocelyn.

All the fear that Sebastian had felt when he'd seen Jocelyn's carriage in front of the Blackstones' townhouse came rushing back to him, and he turned his gaze out the window, not wanting Blackstone to see his inner turmoil.

Two things had become clear to him in the moment he'd known she was in danger. One, he loved her, and love wasn't at all the smoke and mirrors sort of trickery he'd always imagined it to be. He wanted to cherish her and keep her safe as much as he wanted to make love to her. Two, he couldn't go on like this. Not if she was never going to love him in return.

JOCELYN HAD JUST SETTLED Oliver into bed for the night when Winston met her in the hallway outside the nursery. "Inspector Ness is here, my lady. He's waiting for you in the sitting room."

Her heart gave a glad thud, and she couldn't control the smile that broke out on her face. He'd come! She'd so hoped he would. "Thank you, Winston."

She thought about stopping by her bedroom to check her appearance and freshen up, but her need to throw herself into the protection of his strong arms trumped her vanity. She raced down the stairs, screeching to a halt outside the sitting room doors. Taking a deep breath, she made an effort to compose herself, then went inside.

Sebastian had been standing by the window, but when she entered, he crossed the room to her side, kicking the door shut with his foot and then pulling her into a fierce embrace. "I was so worried about you."

"I'm so sorry," she said, burying her face against his chest, which still held some of the chill from outside but also his unique scent. "I shouldn't have gone there. I know that now."

"You've taken good security measures," he told her approvingly. "I was glad to see that when I arrived. And Blackstone is going to put a man on your house until we bring Danbury to justice. I don't think he'll come here, but you must promise me you won't go anywhere alone."

"I promise," she assured him, glad that he wasn't taking her to task for being so foolish in the first place. "I'm so glad you've come. I was hoping you would."

"When I saw you there..." He shook his head, his gaze haunted. "I've never felt such fear."

Her heart thrilled at his concern even as she felt overwhelmed with guilt for causing it. She lifted her face toward his, about to apologize once again, but before she could, he covered her mouth with his, kissing her with fierce possession.

All her thoughts fell away as she wrapped her arms around him and kissed him back just as hungrily. In his arms, she felt as though nothing could hurt her.

Just when she thought he'd lay her down on the sofa and truly make everything else fade away, he broke away, breathing heavily. Taking a few steps away from her, he ran a trembling hand through his hair.

"I can't..." He shook his head, meeting her gaze, and what she saw in his blue eyes took her breath away, and not in a good way. "I can't do this with you anymore, Jocelyn."

"Do what?" she asked, but she was very afraid she knew.

"This afternoon, when I saw you at the Blackstones' townhouse, my fear for you was so intense that it made me realize how much I care for you."

Her heart swelled at his words, but they belied the look in his eyes, and confusion filled her. She tried to respond but before she could think what to say, he held up his hand. "I care for you too much to keep taking from you this way. To risk getting you with child when you've made it so clear that you don't want to marry me. You don't want my child."

*But I do!*

As she stared into his beautiful, beloved face, she realized that even though she'd sworn she'd never fall in love, had been so certain she never wanted to marry again, she hadn't taken into account that she'd meet someone like Sebastian Ness. She knew that he'd never hurt her, that she could trust him with all that she had. A union with this man would be a joy, not a prison.

His face gentled, and he reached out and cupped her face. "But I have to thank you, because you made me realize that I don't want to be alone anymore. I want to share my life with someone. I want to start a family. It wouldn't be fair to either of us if we continue on as we have."

"What are you saying?" she asked, feeling dizzy at the thought of him marrying someone else. "You don't want to see me anymore?"

"I'll never stop wanting to see you," he said softly. "I love you, Jocelyn. But I'm letting you go. I understand why you want your freedom, but I want more than an occasional tumble. I will not be anyone's dalliance, not even yours."

The fact that he'd felt used by her was startling, but she realized that the things she'd said the other morning had made him feel that sex was all she wanted from him. She stared at him, tears filling her eyes, as she struggled to find the words to tell him what he meant to her.

"Don't cry," he said, his voice pained. "The last thing I want is to hurt you. But it's too hard for me to continue like this, given how I feel." He closed the distance between them and kissed her tenderly on the forehead. "I want you to be happy, darling."

With that, he turned and headed toward the door, and she realized that this was it. He was truly leaving her. If he walked out that door, she'd probably never see him again.

Was her need to retain her independence worth losing him?

"Stop," she cried, finally able to speak. "If you walk away from me, I don't think I'll ever be happy again."

He paused, his hand on the door, but he didn't turn around. "You will," he said, his voice strangled. "If all you really want is a lover, there are many men who'd be more than happy to provide that for you."

"I don't want anyone else." She strode toward him and wrapped her arms around him from behind, finding him stiff and unyielding. "You're the only one I've ever wanted, Sebastian. I love you, too."

He turned in her arms, tilting her face up to his. "Do you mean that?" he demanded. "Don't say it if it isn't true."

The vulnerability in his eyes made her wonder if anyone had ever said those words to him in his entire life.

"I love you," she whispered again. "I love you so much. I want to be with you all the time and have your babies. We can figure this out. We can find a solution that works for both of us, don't you think?"

In answer, he kissed her, a kiss filled with such promise and tenderness that her knees threatened to buckle beneath her. She kissed him back with all the love in her heart, all that she'd been holding back for fear that it wouldn't be appreciated. This kiss sealed the beginning of something new, something she knew she'd never regret.

Still kissing her, he swept her up in his arms as though she weighed nothing and carried her over to the sofa, laying her down upon it and then coming down on top of her, his muscular body pressing her against the cushions. She could feel the rigid heat of his desire against her abdomen.

"Is this all right?" he asked, his hands busy beneath her skirts. "I need to be inside you, darling."

"Yes, please," she breathed, lifting her hips to help him

move the heavy fabric out of the way, wishing they were once again naked, skin to skin. But that would take too long, and she wanted exactly what he did. She wanted him now.

A few seconds later, he was rubbing the blunt head of his cock at the seam of her sex, wet with her body's hot arousal, until she was gasping and sobbing his name, begging him to enter her. And then he did so, filling her completely with his thick, hot length, and their gazes met and held.

"I love you," he said again, his heart in his eyes.

"I love you, too," she replied, knowing she'd remember this moment for the rest of her life.

SEBASTIAN LAY UPON his back on Jocelyn's elegant sofa, Jocelyn sprawled across him in glorious dishabille, his heart still pounding in his chest from his release. He'd been so prepared to let her go, he still couldn't believe that she'd told him she didn't want him to.

She'd said she loved him.

He was almost afraid to look at her for fear that he'd somehow misunderstood her. For now, he was content to simply toy with a strand of her beautiful auburn hair and enjoy the moment. If his life never got any better than this moment, he could die a happy man.

"That was lovely," she said at last, her own breathing still somewhat unsteady.

He smiled at her prim and proper way of describing something so decidedly unproper and pressed a tender kiss to her temple. "It certainly was."

Lifting her head, she looked down at him, a look of wonder

in her eyes. "You love me," she said softly, as though she still couldn't believe it either.

"You love me," he countered.

"I do," she agreed. "Maybe I have since the first day we spent together. I've never known anyone like you, Sebastian. You make me feel safe and desired. You make me feel more like myself than I've ever felt before."

He hugged her tightly, humbled and thrilled by her words. "I don't think anyone's ever looked at me the way you do. You make me want to be a better man. You make me want to start a family, to actually live my life, instead of merely surviving it."

They stared at each other for a long moment, understanding flaring between them. He'd been so certain that love was a physical craving, but this connection between them went far deeper than that.

She lowered her head back to his chest, idly toying with the buttons of his vest, making him wish they'd taken the time to undress. "What I said about marriage... I think I've told you enough about mine to the earl for you to know how terrible it was for me. I didn't think I'd ever want to go through that again, convinced myself that I could be happy just taking you as my lover. I thought I could be wild and decadent, pursuing my own pleasure, but I'm not that sort of woman. I missed you the moment I left your arms the other day."

Relief washed through him, and he realized this was exactly what he'd needed to hear from her. He didn't want her to concede to his wishes simply because she didn't want to lose him. He wanted her to want to marry him as well.

"I know I don't have anything to offer—"

She lifted her head again and pressed her fingertips to his

lips. "I don't want to hear that. You have more to offer than I ever even imagined. You're strong, intelligent, tender, an incredible lover." She gave him an impish smile. "Need I go on?"

"I'm not a wealthy man," he told her stubbornly. "I can never give you everything you're accustomed to."

She gestured around the lavish room. "Most of this belongs to Oliver, but I do have some money of my own. Albert left me very comfortable, and until Oliver reaches his majority, it's my duty to raise him in the style he deserves. Would it be so terrible for you to leave your flat in Bethnal Green and move in here?"

He sighed, thinking of the compromise O'Brien and Allison had reached. Quinn had moved up a bit, and Allison had moved down, meeting at a happy medium. But Sebastian had fallen in love with a bloody countess, the guardian of the future Earl of Aston. He could never expect her to move her young son to his hovel in Bethnal Green. He couldn't even ask her to raise the little earl in a place that was somewhere in the middle.

"It would not be terrible at all," he said, realizing how ridiculous it was to protest such a fantastic change in circumstances. "I just never want you to think that I fell in love with you because of all of this. I'd love you if you didn't have a penny to your name."

"I believe you," she said simply.

"Your reputation will suffer," he said, feeling a masochistic need to point out every drawback he could think of. He didn't want her to ever regret her choice and needed her to go into it with her eyes wide open.

"Allison and her brothers weathered the storm, and they've created their own little society. We'll look to them for friendship and socialization. Who cares what anyone else thinks?" She pressed a gentle kiss on his lips. "It's a whole new century. It's time that men were measured for their achievements and their character, not their breeding."

He held her gaze. "You are the most amazing woman I've ever known."

She grinned. "You're pretty wonderful yourself, Inspector."

This was really happening. His beautiful countess was actually going to marry him. It still seemed unreal.

"You won't regret this," he vowed. "I will spend the rest of my life doing my best to make you happy."

"As will I," she said simply.

Silence fell between them once again, but this time, peace filled him. They still had a lot of things to work out between them, and he didn't expect that it would be entirely easy. Hard times would come, but he had found a woman who was more than prepared to weather the storm, who wouldn't run away at the first drop of rain.

"What happened after I left Danbury's?" she asked just as he was about to drift off to sleep. "You said Drake was going to put a man on my house, so I assume you spoke to him."

He sighed, hugging her tight. "I did. I showed him the evidence I had, and he suspects his brother as well, but there just isn't enough proof yet to go after him. He has a plan, and I don't have any choice but to go along with it."

She shivered. "I can't believe that Mortimer Blackstone is The Viper. He killed Evelyn... Why? Because she rejected him years ago? But when I looked in his eyes, I knew. He's truly evil.

There's nothing left in him of the boy I once knew."

"We'll make him pay for it," he assured her, though he wasn't at all certain. So much rested in Blackstone's hands, and he still didn't know if he trusted his boss's loyalties. But right now, all he could do was keep the woman he loved safe.

For tonight, that was enough.

# Epilogue

July 1910

Sebastian stood on the fence rail, watching his children ride their horses around the paddock at Summer Hill, their country estate in Kent. His family didn't get up here nearly as much as he'd like, given the demands of his job as the new assistant police commissioner and the work Jocelyn did with the women's suffrage movement, but they all enjoyed their time in the country whenever they could get it.

"Daddy, watch me!" cried Evelyn, his six-year-old daughter, as she bounced along on her pony, grinning from ear to ear. She had her mother's auburn hair but the serious bookish temperament of the aunt she'd been named after. They could rarely get her nose out of a book, but she became another creature entirely when it came to horses.

"He *is* watching you!" said Oliver, who was coming into his own as a young man of eleven. He rode a beautiful sorrel mare, his seat perfect, the bright sunlight catching in his golden hair.

In the beginning, Sebastian had been worried that his stepson would resent him, or that he'd never find a true connection with him, but his fears had been unfounded. Oliver had taken to him immediately, and he loved the boy every bit as much as he did the children he'd sired. He felt blessed to have the opportunity to help mold the young earl into the powerful man he'd someday be. He and Jocelyn had done their best to show him more than just the glittering aristocracy to which he'd been born.

"I see you, sweetie," Sebastian called to his daughter. "I'm watching you all!"

"Look at me!" shouted four-year-old Peter, who was also on a pony but had a young groom walking beside him to ensure that he remained seated. Little Peter took after his father, with dark hair and blue eyes, but he had his mother's sunny personality.

"They love this. I wish we could spend more time here."

Sebastian turned around to find Jocelyn had come up behind him, carrying their little blonde daughter Marilyn, who'd just turned one and was too young for riding. He jumped off the fence and pulled his wife into a one-armed hug, then tapped Marilyn on the nose. The baby laughed uproariously.

"Yeah, me, too." But he knew she didn't seriously want their life to be anything except what it was. Sometimes chaotic, always busy, but filled with the things and the people they loved.

"I wish Evelyn could see our family," Jocelyn said unexpectedly, her gaze focused on their children. She rarely talked about her sister, but he knew Evelyn was never far from her thoughts. He was glad he'd been able to see Evelyn's killer brought to justice, even though he still had nightmares of the months leading up to The Viper's capture.

"I think she's watching," he said. "I certainly feel that we've had a guardian angel looking after us over the years."

Things hadn't always been easy. They'd faced plenty of scorn and ridicule for their uneven match, especially in the beginning. But Jocelyn had never seemed to mind, and he certainly didn't give a damn what people thought.

Jocelyn nodded, blinking away a sheen of tears, then smiled up at him. "We're luckier than most, that's for certain. I'm well aware of my blessings."

He smiled. "Do you remember the first conversation we ever had? Where we both smugly asserted that love didn't exist?"

Jocelyn laughed, the happy sound making all four of their children laugh as well. "We had no idea what we were talking about, did we?"

"We certainly didn't, and I've never in my life been so happy to be wrong." The love he received every day, not just from Jocelyn but from his children and the extended family they'd created with their friends, filled his cup until it ran over in the most magical ways.

THE END

WILL DRAKE BLACKSTONE be able to stop his brother before he kills again?

Will Heather Fields' dangerous activities get in the way of Drake's carefully laid plans?

Read DARK DESIRES, the next chapter in Diana Bold's UNMASKING PROMETHEUS series!

When Mandrake Blackstone, the assistant police commissioner, begins to suspect that his older brother, Viscount Danbury, is the notorious killer The Viper, he is determined to bring him to justice. But he has no proof, and one can't just arrest a member of the *ton* without being certain. But when he is trapped in an explosion with lovely Heather Fields, he begins to question everything, including the code of ethics that was once so clear to him.

I hope you enjoyed reading Sebastian and Jocelyn's story as much as I enjoyed writing it! If you did, I would greatly appreciate a short review where you purchased it or your favorite book website. Reviews are crucial for any author, and even just a sentence or two can make a huge difference.

*Diana Bold has been writing since elementary school and never wanted to be anything but a writer. It took longer than she hoped to accomplish that, but she is now the award-winning author of more than thirty historical romances. She lives in the mountains of Southern Colorado with the love of her life, whom she met rather late in life but was worth the wait. When she's not writing, she enjoys traveling and genealogy.*

# Don't miss out!

Visit the website below and you can sign up to receive emails whenever Diana Bold publishes a new book. There's no charge and no obligation.

https://books2read.com/r/B-A-QJSG-OSLTB

**BOOKS 2 READ**

Connecting independent readers to independent writers.